박윤주, 찰스윤의 스토리가 있는 영어 I

박윤주 · 찰스윤 공저

에피스테메
EPISTEME

박윤주 · 찰스윤의 스토리가 있는 영어 Ⅰ

ⓒ 박윤주 · 찰스윤, 2011

초판 1쇄 펴낸날 / 2011년 2월 21일
초판 2쇄 펴낸날 / 2013년 3월 30일

지은이 / 박윤주 · 찰스윤
펴낸이 / 조남철
펴낸곳 / (사)한국방송통신대학교출판부
　　　　주소　서울특별시 종로구 이화장길 54 (110-500)
　　　　대표전화 1644-1232
　　　　팩스 (02) 742-0956
　　　　http://press.knou.ac.kr
　　　　출판등록 1982년 6월 7일 제1-491호

편집 · 조판 / 하람커뮤니케이션
일러스트 / 박완기
인쇄 / 한국소문사

ISBN 978-89-20-00423-0 93840
값 12,000원

　　TV 방송과 수업에 이어, 교재로 인사를 드립니다. 『스토리가 있는 영어 I 』을 집필하면서, 한국에서 영어를 공부하는 우리의 상황을 최대한 반영한, '생생하게 살아있는 영어'를 전하고자 노력하였습니다. 우리를 반영한 주인공들, 그리고 그들을 둘러싼 다양한 국가의 친구들을 통해, 여러분들은 실제로 영어를 사용하는 상황을 자연스럽게 마주칠 수 있을 것입니다. 주인공들의 첫 만남에서 데이트, 직업과 공부의 병행, 친구들과의 만남이나 여행까지 본 교재는 여러 등장인물의 일상생활을 중심으로 꾸며졌습니다.

　　내용상의 특성을 살펴보면, 각 장은 Key Patterns, Alternative Expressions, Focus on Pronunciation, Real & Live, Exercises로 구성되어 있습니다. 우선 Key Patterns를 통해서 여러분은 '나를 중심으로 하는 발화 I-Expression' 다양한 종류의 '평서문', 그리고 유용한 '의문문' 표현을 익히실 수 있습니다. 대화문의 문장 가운데에서 흥미로운 표현 5가지를 골라 엮은 Alternative Expressions는 여러분의 어휘와 문장 수준을 한 단계 높여줄 것입니다. "이런 한국어 표현은 어떻게 말하지?"라는 궁금증은 Real & Live를 통해 풀어보세요. 그리고 늘 언제나 재미있는 Exercises로 마무리하시기 바랍니다. 주제별로 엮은 Culture Corner는 미국 문화에 대한 유익한 읽을거리, 생각할 거리를 제공할 것입니다.

　　교재의 처음부터 끝까지 애써준 성지연, 서정인, 최영임 선생님 고마워요. 독특한 그림으로 책을 꾸며준 박완기 선생님 감사합니다. 그러나 이 책의 완성은 구입해서 닳도록 듣고, 보고, 읽고, 쓰면서 자신의 것으로 만드는 여러분에게 달려 있습니다. 이 교재가 여러분을 즐겁고 행복한 영어회화의 길로 안내하길 진심으로 바랍니다.

박윤주

It can be challenging to capture the natural flow of conversational English while simultaneously deepening one's understanding of the sometimes hidden nuances, contexts and culture of a language. This book was written with the idea that context is a key part to language learning. As an introduction to English, we have included key expressions, structures, and exercises in pronunciation and syntax. In addition, students may find alternative expressions and cultural notes to engage their interest and add deeper context to their understanding. The authors have tried to select useful, practical expressions taken from everyday life and then situate them in contexts that students can relate to.

Unlike many other English conversation books that take place exclusively in the United States and use mainly American characters, this book tried to keep the identity and corresponding needs of Korean students in mind. Also, given the reality of a vibrant, transnational Seoul, the authors aimed to create contexts and common situations experienced by a diverse set of native Korean and expatriate characters living in South Korea. The hope was that by grounding the dialogues and exercises within a transnational context, the book would better reflect the intercultural reality of English usage in South Korea today. It is the authors' sincere hope that students will find this book to be both practical and helpful in their studies.

Acknowledgments must be given to Jiyeon Sung, JungIn Seo, and Yeong-im Choi whose help was invaluable to this book. The authors would also like to thank the many friends and colleagues who proofread and reviewed the materials in order to make this work possible.

Charse Yun

Contents

Scope and Sequence

Themes	Lessons	Key Patterns	Focus on Pronunciation	Real & Live	Culture Corner
I Meeting	1 Introducing Friends	• I'm ~. • Let's ~. • What's ~ like?	• Content words & Function words	• Do you have (some) time? • Do you have a business card? • got her/his digits!	Names
	2 Getting to Know You	• I'm happy ~. • You're such a ~. • What kind of ~ do you like?	• Stress-timed English vs. Syllable timed Korean	• She's a hottie. • He's a catch. • Hook me up with her/him.	
II Dating	3 Blind Date	• I love ~. • Thanks for ~. • What do you think about ~?	• 강세를 받는 모음 a, e, i의 발음	• Go get her/him. • Somebody hit her/him with an ugly stick. • I used to be hot.	Football
	4 Going to the Performance	• I was impressed. • That sounds like ~! • Why don't we ~?	• o, u의 발음과 애매모음	• I'll get this. • That's terrible. vs. That rocks. • You have good taste in music.	
III Working Life	5 Confirming the Meeting	• I would like to ~. • We have ~. • When ~?	• 모음 사이의 x의 발음	• How are you doing on that project? • I'm on top of it. • I have a full plate.	Money
	6 Shopping	• I'll ~. • It's quite crowded. • How much ~	• 구개음화	• It's in. • What a deal! • It's a must-have (item).	
	7 Hangover	• I can't ~. • either ~ or ~. • Why ~?	• th의 발음	• Cheers! • I threw up what I ate. • My stomach is killing me.	

IV Studying	8 Pronunciation Problems!	• I said ~. • It's ~ to ~. • What are you~ing?	• 일반 동사의 3인칭 현재형 ~s 의 발음	• I (just) don't get it. • I get it. • snacks / munchies	Diversity
	9 Tips for Studying	• I have been ~ing. • If ~ • How do ~?	• 과거형 ~ed의 발음	• What's your secret? • He's a machine. • Excuse me, haven't I seen you somewhere before?	
V Invitations	10 Inviting Friends	• I'm in. • Nobody ~. • What's up?	• Flapping	• I'm being stood up. • How can you do that to me? • Please put yourself in my shoes.	Holidays
	11 Surprise Party	• I hope ~. • Let me ~. • What brings you here?	• H의 약화	• I had a hunch that you would come today. • I'm flying high. • You're the best!	
	12 Potluck Dinner	• I'm starving! • It is good for~. • Where ~?	• And의 발음	• I'm stuffed. • Everybody chips in. • Let's split this.	
VI Travel	13 Planning Vacations	• I was ~ing. • It's better ~ than ~. • How long ~?	• Stress in Noun/Verb pairs	• Let's take a road trip! • Let's hit the road! • I'm on the road.	Geography
	14 Making Reservations	• I would prefer to~. • That will be ~. • What time ~?	• 접미사와 접두사가 있는 단어의 강세	• Does that include breakfast? • I'm planning to spend the weekend at a B&B. • The clerk is so good to me.	
	15 Saying Good-bye	• I feel ~. • That used to ~. • Where ~?	• 복합어 강세 – 강세에 따른 의미 변화	• It was really good meeting you. • I'm really going to /gonna miss you. • I hope you do well.	

Scope and Sequence   vii

Characters

Soyeong

Jennifer

Michael

Alex

Matthew

Stella

Soyeong	A Korean student who works. She is interested in theater and is friends with Jennifer
Jennifer	A friend of Soyeong's from the U.S.
Michael	A newly arrived theater director from Canada
Alex	A Korean American who works in finance
Matthew	An American who is Jennifer's boyfriend
Stella	A professor of English from Canada

Theme I

Meeting

Lesson 1
Introducing Friends

Lesson 2
Getting to Know You

In Theme I, Soyeong accidentally runs into Jennifer and Michael in front of the subway station in the Daehangno neighborhood of Seoul. Soyeong is a Korean university student and Michael is a theater director from Canada. Jennifer is the mutual friend from New York who introduces the two of them. After being introduced, Soyeong and Michael continue their conversation in a coffee shop. There, Michael offers to arrange a blind date for Soyeong with his friend Alex, a Korean American who works in the financial industry in Seoul.

Introducing Friends

• At the subway entrance

Soyeong Jennifer! **What are you doing here?**

Jennifer Hi, Soyeong! I'm just here to meet a friend. Let me introduce you. Michael, this is my former Korean instructor.

Soyeong Hi, I'm Soyeong. It's nice to meet you.

Michael My name is Michael. Nice to meet you, Soyeong. **What do you do here in Seoul?**

Soyeong **I'm a student at** Korea National Open University.

Michael Your English is quite good! Have you ever lived in the States or Canada by chance?

Soyeong I've studied in Arizona in the U.S. for three years.

Michael Arizona! That's interesting! What's Arizona like?

Soyeong **It was very hot!** But I liked it a lot.

Jennifer You know, we should meet again and talk some more. Let's all get together for coffee sometime.

Michael That's a great idea! **Here's my business card.**

Soyeong Thanks!

Key Patterns

1. I'm _____.   I'm *Soyeong*
2. Let's _____.
   Let's *all get together for coffee sometime.*
3. What's _____ like?   **What's** *Arizona* **like?**

1

I'm _____.   나는 _____ 입니다.
I'm Soyeong.

세상의 중심은 누구인가요? 다양한 답이 가능하겠지만, 저는 "자신"이라고 답하겠습니다. 자신을 소개할 때 간단히 "I'm _____"이라고 하는 것이 "My name is _____"라고 하는 것보다 더 자연스럽습니다.

A. "I'm ~"으로 시작하는 문장은 모든 회화의 기본입니다.

I'm + 명사: I'm a student at Korea National Open University.
　　　　　　저는 한국방송통신대학교 학생입니다.
I'm + to 동사원형: I'm here to meet a friend.   저는 친구를 만나려고 왔어요.
I'm + 전치사: I'm from Seoul.   저는 서울이 고향이에요.

2

Let's _____.   우리 같이 _____ 합시다.
Let's all get together for coffee sometime.

Let us + 동사원형이 오는 문형입니다. Let's 는 무엇을 함께 하자고 권할 때 사용할

4

수 있는 가장 유용한 표현이죠. 한국어로 쉽게 "~합시다"라고 이해하시면 됩니다.

A. Let's + 동사원형: 가장 기본입니다. 여기서처럼 Let's + get (together). '우리 함께 모이자' 가 되겠지요.

Let's go home.   우리 집에 갑시다.

B. Let's 동사원형 + for: 'for + 대상' 즉, 무언가를 목적으로 해서 뭔가를 하자고 하는 표현입니다. 본문에 나온 표현으로 Let's + get (together) + for coffee! 하면 '커피를 마시러 모이자' 가 되는 거죠.

Let's go for a walk.   우리 산책 갑시다.

3

What's _____ like?   _____ 는 어떤가요?
What's Arizona like?

Wh-의문문의 첫 번째 표현으로 등장한 "What's _____ like?"는 "_____ 는 어때요?/어떤가요?"라는 뜻으로, 상대편의 의견을 묻는 상황에 사용합니다. 특히 단순한 의견에 대한 질문이라기보다는 뭔가 경험한 것에 대한 의견을 묻는다는 점을 기억하세요. Michael이 소영에게 "Arizona는 어때요?"라고 질문한 상황은, 소영이 3년간 살다 온 곳에 대한 경험을 묻는다고 할 수 있겠습니다.

What's Christmas like in the U.S.?
미국에서의 크리스마스는 어때요?
What's it like to work and study (at the same time)?
일하면서 공부를 병행하는 것이 어떻습니까?

Alternative Expressions

1   What are you doing here?

= *What brings you here?*

= *Funny running into you here!*

2   What do you do here in Seoul?

= *What do you do here?*

= *What do you do for a living?*

= *What line of work are you in?*

3   I am a student at~

= *I majored in (subject).*

= *I studied (subject).*

4   It was very hot.

= *It was very*

hot	*dry*	*overcast*
humid	*rainy*	*foggy*
muggy	*cold*	*windy*
chilly	*warm*	*sunny*

5   Here's my business card.

What's your cell phone number?

You can also e-mail me.

Let me have your cell phone number and I'll call you.

I'd be happy to discuss it with you sometime.

I'd be happy to discuss it whenever you're free.

What's your cell phone number?

Focus on Pronunciation

● Part 1. 언 어

1. Content Words(내용어) & Function Words(기능어)

자연스럽게 이야기하기 위해서는 음절 하나 하나의 발음, 단어의 강세, 문장의 억양 등 영어의 다양한 요소를 고려해야 합니다. 제1과에서는 단어와 문장의 강세, 억양에 대해서 알아보는데, 이를 이해하기 위한 가장 중요한 요소가 내용어와 기능어에 대한 이해입니다.

한국어는 문장의 단어들을 같은 억양으로 발음하는 반면, 영어는 중요한 단어(내용어)는 강하게 발음하고 중요하지 않은 단어(기능어)는 약하게 발음합니다. 이를 나누어보면 아래와 같습니다.

❶ content words(내용어) : noun (명사), adjective (형용사), verb (동사),
                          adverb (부사)

❷ functional words(기능어) : pronoun (대명사), preposition (전치사),
                            auxiliary verb (조동사), conjunction (접속사),
                            be-verb (be동사)

예문을 통해 살펴봅시다.

ex) What **do you** do?

의문사에 해당하는 what과 마지막 일반동사의 do가 강하게 발음되겠죠?
앞의 do는 조동사인 기능어이므로 약하게 발음하고 뒤의 do는 동사로 내용어이므로 강하게 발음합니다.

이번에는 본문 속 예문들입니다. 큰 소리로 읽어보시기 바랍니다.

It's nice to meet you. (nice, meet)

I'm from Seoul, but I studied in Arizona in the U.S. for three years.
(Seoul, studied, Arizona, U.S. three years)

괄호 안에 들어 있는 단어들이 내용어에 해당하므로, 강하게 발음됩니다.

Real & Live는 구어적인 한국어 표현이 영어로는 어떻게 표현되는지 알아보는 장입니다. 각 표현들을 간단한 대화를 통해 자연스럽게 익힐 수 있도록 노력하세요.

1. (혹시) 시간 있으세요? Do you have (some) time?

맘에 드는 사람이 나타났을 때 사용할 수 있는 전형적인 pickup line 표현입니다. 가장 주의하실 점은 이 경우, 절대로 정관사 the를 사용하지 않는다는 겁니다. 정관사 없이 time 혹은 some time을 사용해야, "시간 있으세요?"라는 뜻이 됩니다. 정관사를 사용해서 "Do you have the time?"으로 물어보면 "몇 시예요?"라는 전혀 다른 뜻이 됩니다. 물론 약속을 잡기 위해서 시간이 있는지 확인하기 위한 표현으로도 사용됩니다. "Do you have some time this Friday? I'd like to meet with you to discuss something important"처럼 말이죠.

> A: Hey Jane, I was wondering. Do you have some time this Friday evening? I'd like to take you out to dinner.
> B: Sure, I'd love to. Pick me up around 7?

2. (혹시) 명함 있으세요? Do you have a business card?

자신을 소개하는 데에는 명함을 건네는 것만큼 빠르고 쉬운 방법이 없겠죠? 명함은 영어로 "business card"라고 합니다. 종종 명함을 "name card"라고 하는 분들도 있는데요, 완전히 틀린 표현은 아니지만 명함에는 이름(name)만 있는 게 아니기에 "business card"라고 하는 것이 정확한 표현입니다. 상대방에게 명함을 요구하는 좀 더 정중한 표현으로 "May I get/have your business card, please?"를 쓰셔도 좋습니다.

A: I'd like to discuss this with you further.
   Do you have a business card?
B: Of course. Here it is.

3. 번호 땄어! I got her/his digits!

보통 전화번호는 phone number 혹은 그냥 number라고 많이 알고 계시죠? 물론 이 표현들도 정확하고 유용합니다. 여기에 하나 더 재밌는 표현을 알려 드릴게요. 번호를 나타내는 표현으로 "digit"을 사용하기도 한답니다. "digit"은 아라비아 숫자를 의미하는데요, 전화번호가 모두 아라비아 숫자로만 되어 있기에 이런 표현도 사용하실 수 있는 거죠.

A: So Jim, what happened after you met that girl last night?
B: I got digits! I will call her tomorrow.

Exercises

• Select the Appropriate Word

1. What's Arizona _____ ?
   a. like   b. likes

2. Your English is _____ good!
   a. yet   b. quite

3. I'm just here _____ a friend.
   a. meeting   b. to meet

4. What _____ you do here in Seoul?
   a. do   b. are

5. I'm a student _____ Korea National Open University.
   a. at   b. in

6. _____ all get together for coffee sometime.
   a. Just   b. Let's

7. I studied in Arizona in the U.S _____ three years.
   a. for   b. since

Getting to Know You

Jennifer Hi, guys. Sorry I'm late.

Soyeong That's OK. Where are you coming from?

Jennifer I just met my boyfriend in Itaewon for lunch. I didn't know there would be such a traffic jam!

Michael I didn't know you were seeing someone! Do you have your boyfriend's picture?

Jennifer Sure, I have one on my cell phone.

Soyeong **You and your boyfriend look so cute together.** I'm so happy for you!

Michael What about you? **You're not seeing anyone?**

Soyeong No, **I'm still available.** I wish I had a boyfriend!

Jennifer I'm sure you'll meet someone. You're such a catch. Are you interested in anyone?

Soyeong Well, I don't have my eye on anyone, but I'm looking around.

Michael If you're interested in meeting someone, I might be able to set you up. What kind of guy do you like?

1. I'm _____.   I'm happy for you.
2. You're such a _____.   You're such a catch.
3. What kind of _____?   What kind of guy do you like?

1

I'm _____.   나는 _____ 합니다.
I'm happy for you.

I'm + 형용사: 자신의 현재 상태나 상황을 말하고 싶을 때 가장 유용한 표현입니다.
I'm 다음에 형용사를 넣어서 감정을 표현해볼까요?

I'm + happy (for you!)   당신 상황에 대해 저는 기뻐요!
(I'm) Sorry I'm late.   늦어서 미안해요.
I'm (still) available.   저 싱글이에요 or 저 시간 있습니다.
I'm sure you'll meet someone.   저는 당신이 누군가를 만날 것으로 확신합니다.

2

You're such a _____.   당신은 정말 _____ 하군요.
You're such a catch.

상대편의 상황이나 상태는 그럼 I'm을 응용해 You're이라고 하면 되겠죠?

A. You're + 명사 혹은 You're + 형용사 표현이 가능합니다.

You're + 명사: You're (such) a catch.   당신 (이렇게) 괜찮은 사람인데요.
You're + 형용사: You're interested in meeting someone.
당신은 누군가를 만나는 것에 관심이 있으시군요.

14

B. such (a/an) + 형용사 + 명사 형태: Such (a/an) 도 중요한 표현입니다. "이렇게/
그렇게/매우/그러한" 등의 뜻을 갖고 있으며 문법으로만 익히시지 말고, 회화에서 활
용할 수 있도록 노력해봅시다!

There's no such thing as magic! 마술 같은 일은 없어!
She has such a beautiful face. 그녀 얼굴은 너무나 아름다워.

3

What kind of _____? 어떤 종류의 ____를 _____하죠?
What kind of guy do you like?

"What kind of~?" 표현은 "어떤 종류의 ~를 ~하시나요?"라는 문장입니다. 많은
사람들이 kind of와 sort of가 같다고 생각하는데, 위와 같은 문장의 경우 sort of로
바꿔 사용하지 않습니다. Sort가 kind보다 다소 구어적으로 가볍게 느껴지기 때문이
죠. 처음부터 What kind of~의 문형으로 외워서 사용하시기 바랍니다.

What kind of guy do you like? 어떤 남자를 좋아해?
What kind of music (does he play)? 그는 어떤 음악을 연주하죠?
What kind of car (do you drive)? 어떤 종류의 차를 운전하십니까?

Alternative Expressions

1 You and your boyfriend look so cute together.
= *You make a cute couple!*
Lovebirds = a couple who are clearly in love

2 I'm still available.
= *I'm interested in meeting people.*
= *I'm looking around!*
= *I'm on the market!*

3 You are not seeing anyone?
= *Has anyone caught your eye?*
= *Anyone special?*
= *Are you interested in meeting anyone?*
= *Anyone on the horizon?*

4 What kind of guy do you like?
= *What do you look for in a guy/girl?*
= *What kind of girl/guy do you go for?*
= *What qualities do you look for in a guy/girl/date?*

5 What kind of guy do you like?
Responses: *I like*   *tall*   *intelligent*   *considerate*
                      shy   *nerdy*   *masculine*
                      feminine   *handsome*   *beautiful*

I'm into *tall girls.*
I go for *"bad boys."*

2. Stress-timed English(강세박자)
vs Syllable-timed Korean(음절박자)

stress(강세)와 syllable(음절)이라는 개념 역시 영어를 문장 단위로 말할 때 매우 중요합니다. 영어는 강세박자 언어에 속하기 때문에 중요한 단어에만 강세를 주어 발음하는 반면, 우리말은 음절박자 언어기 때문에 모든 음절마다 강세를 주어서 발음합니다. 즉, 영어는 내용어와 기능어에 대한 구분이 있기 때문에 강세를 중요 시하고 그에 따라 잘 들리고, 잘 들리지 않는 단어가 있습니다. 그러나 한국어는 내용어와 기능어 발음에 대한 차이가 상대적으로 적기 때문에, 모든 단어를 발음 하는 것처럼 느껴집니다.

Birds	eat	corn.
The birds	eat	corn.
The birds	can eat	corn.
The birds	can eat	the corn.

새가	옥수수를	먹는다			
그	새가	옥수수를	먹는다		
그	새가	옥수수를	먹을	수	있다
그	새가	그	옥수수를	먹을	수	있다

영어는 중요한 단어만 강세를 주어 발음하기 때문에 네 문장의 길이를 같게 발 음하지만, 우리말은 모든 음절에 강세를 주어 발음하기 때문에 점점 길게 발음 합니다.

1. 멋진 여성에게 하는 말 She's a hottie.

눈이 돌아갈 정도로 멋진 여성을 봤을 때 이렇게 표현할 수 있습니다. 아니면 hottie 대신에 babe를 쓸 수도 있는데, 이때 baby가 아니라 babe라는 차이점을 확인하시고 발음에 유의하셔야 합니다. 또한 "She's sweet/nice/pure/wholesome"과 같은 다양한 표현이 있으니 함께 알아두시면 좋겠죠? 이밖에 "She's like a girl next door."라는 문장 역시 멋진 여성에 대한 표현인데, 한국어로 '옆집 순이'는 예쁘다기보다는 그저 편한 여성의 느낌이 강한데, 영어로 이웃집 소녀처럼 예쁘다는 것은 정말 멋지다는 것이니, 익혀둘 만한 표현이죠?

A: Hey Bill, what do you think of Jennifer?
B: Jennifer? She's a hottie! She's very popular among the guys.

2. 멋진 남성에게 하는 말 He's a catch.

이번엔 남성에 대한 표현을 알아볼까요? "catch"라는 표현은 보통 동사로 "잡다"라는 의미로 많이 쓰는데요, 명사로 "a catch"라고 쓰게 되면 잡을 만큼 괜찮은 사람이라는 의미가 됩니다. 하지만 이 표현은 slang으로 격식을 차려야 하는 자리에서는 사용에 주의하세요!

A: Jill, what do you think of Steve?
B: He's such a catch. He's tall, handsome and very intelligent.

3. 좋은 사람 있으면 소개해줘. Hook me up with her/him.

Hook는 금속이나 플라스틱으로 만든 고리를 뜻합니다. 고리로 누군가와 누군가를 연결시킨다는 표현으로 주로 '소개해주다'는 동사구로 많이 사용됩니다. 남녀의 데이트를 위해 서로를 소개해주는 경우, 혹은 좀 더 구어적으로 남, 녀간의 성적인 표현으로 사용될 수도 있습니다. 또한 격식을 차린 자리로 부모님이나 어른을 만나서 시간을 보내는 경우에도 이 표현을 사용할 수 있습니다.

● Hook me up with your dad so I can get a job.
(나를 너의 아버지께 소개시켜줘 그럼 내가 취업이나 뭐 좀 할 수 있지 않을까.)

A: Susan, I need to invest some money in the stock market.
   Do you think you could hook me up with a good broker?
B: Sure, I'd be happy to.

Exercises

• Match Up Words and Meaning

Words	Meaning

Words **Meaning**

1. late   A. Something that is related to the past

2. "a catch"   B. Attracts your attention, or appeals to you

3. former   C. A slang term that means an ideal partner

4. picture   D. Tell each other's names in order to know each other

5. available   E. After the time that was arranged or expected

6. introduce   F. Not busy and therefore free to talk, meet or to do a particular task, etc.

7. interesting   G. A small card given to other people which indicates name and contact information

8. boyfriend   H. A long line of vehicles on a street or highway that cannot move quickly because there are too many cars

9. traffic jam   I. A male that is in a relationship with a female

10. business card   J. Shapes which are drawn, painted, or printed on a surface and show a person, thing, or scene

Culture Corner

• Names

In the United States, there are a great variety of names reflecting the tremendous diversity of the population. Interestingly, however, the majority of names today are still dominated by names of English origin. That is, despite the massive waves of immigration from all over the globe, most American names can be traced to settlers and pilgrims from England.

The Judeo-Christian tradition certainly had a tremendous impact on the history of England, especially during the Middle Ages and during the Protestant Reformation. In fact, the Puritans, who were some of the earliest settlers to America in the 1600s, commonly took their names from the Bible. Even today, one can find many popular names that are found in the Bible such as John, Aaron, Benjamin, Rachel, Ruth, Esther, Isaac, Jacob and Naomi.

According to the U.S. government, some of the most popular names in America in the past decade have been:

Boys	Girls
Jacob	Emily
Michael	Ashley
Joshua	Emma
Matthew	Hannah
Andrew	Elizabeth

Do you know some popular shortened versions for names? Boy names are more commonly shortened than are girl names.

James = Jim or Jake	Elizabeth = Liz, Lisa or Eliza
Michael = Mike	Rebecca = Becca
Frederick = Fred or Eric	Jennifer = Jenny or Jen
Johnathon or Jonathan = John or Jon	Susan = Sue or Susie
Timothy = Tim	Katherine = Kate or Katie
Robert = Bob	Pamela = Pam
William = Bill	Melissa = Missy
Henry = Hank	Christine = Chris or Chrissy

● **Most American names come from what country of origin?**

● **What book did the Puritans take their names from?**

Theme II

Dating

In Theme II, Soyeong meets Alex for the first time at a restaurant and the two enjoy their date together. To their delight, they learn that they both have an interest and passion in theater performances. Inspired, Alex invites Soyeong to see Michael's new play. After seeing the performance, both are very impressed and praise Michael for his success.

Blind Date

Soyeong   This is such a nice restaurant!

Alex   Yes, I like this place a lot. Thanks for coming. It's nice to finally meet you. **I've heard so much about you** from Michael.

Soyeong   Really? I know so little about you! **I hope you don't mind my asking**, but what do you do for a living?

Alex   Actually, I'm in finance.

Soyeong   That must be interesting.

Alex   Well, not really. Even though I work in finance, my real passion is the theater. **What do you do in your free time?**

Soyeong   Oh, I love the theater, too! In fact, I'm a member of a theater group at my university!

Alex   What a coincidence! I also used to do some acting when I was in college. What do you think about musicals?

Soyeong   I love musicals! Michael introduced me to them. I wish I could see them more often.

Alex   Well, you know, Michael gave me two tickets to his new musical that he's directing. It's in Daehangno. Would you like to see a show with me this weekend?

Soyeong   That sounds great. **Let me check my schedule**. I just happen to be free this weekend, too! So **when should we meet?**

Key Patterns

1. I love _____.   I **love** the theater.
2. Thanks for _____.   **Thanks for** coming.
3. What **do you think about** _____?

   What do you think about musicals?

1

I love _____.   저는 _____를 너무 좋아해요.

I love the theater.

Love를 사랑한다는 뜻과 함께, 정말 좋아한다는 뜻으로 익혀두세요. Love 위치에
수많은 동사를 넣어서, 'I + 동사 + 명사' 문형을 사용할 수도 있습니다. 여러분이
알고 있는 그 수많은 영어 동사들을 이 패턴에서 적용시켜 사용해봅시다.

I love musicals!

뮤지컬 진짜 좋아해요!

I love to go to the movies!

영화 보러가는 것을 정말 좋아해.

I really enjoy what I do at work.

내가 하는 일을 정말 즐겨요.

2

Thanks for _____. _____ 에 대해서 감사합니다.
Thanks for coming.

"Thank + 사람 + for ∼ :∼에게 ∼한 것에 관해서 고마움을 느끼다"입니다. Thank you를 Thanks로 바꾼 다음 for + come (∼ing)이 와서 "와줘서 고마워"가 되죠.

Thank you for the gift. 선물 감사합니다.
Thank you (so much) for the ride. 태워줘서 고마워.

A. I appreciate _____. "I appreciate + 명사"는 더 정중한 표현입니다.

I appreciate your assistance. 도와주셔서 감사드려요.
I appreciate your advice. 충고 감사합니다.

B. Thanks to _____. "Thanks to∼"는 더 관용적인 표현으로 '∼덕분입니다' 이며, 책이나 음악 앨범 등에서 저자나 가수가 감사하는 사람들을 적을 때 주로 사용하는 표현입니다. "Thanks to my YJ＊＊ family all over the world"라면 "전세계 YJ＊＊ (∼회사) 가족 여러분 감사드립니다"가 되겠죠. 혹시 이런 표현을 보신 적이 있으신가요?

What do you think about _____?

_____ 에 관해 어떻게 생각하세요?

What do you think about musicals?

"what do you think about~?"는 아주 유용한 표현입니다. About이라는 전치사 다음에 명사형을 넣고, 그것에 대해 어떻게 생각하는지 상대편의 의견을 묻는거죠.

What do you think about studying abroad?

유학에 대해 어떻게 생각하세요?

A. Think about 과 think of 를 구분하고 싶다면 think about이 좀 더 큰 개념에 대해 사용하고, think of는 좀 더 작은 범위, 즉 더 주관적인 입장을 묻는다고 할 수 있습니다. 물론 절대적인 것이 아니고 상대적이라는 점도 미리 밝혀둡니다.

What do you think about musicals?

(일반적인) 뮤지컬을 어떻게 생각해?

What did you think of that musical we saw together?

우리 같이 보고 나온 그 뮤지컬 어땠어?

B. What do you think 다음에 절(주어+동사형)이 오는 경우도 생각해봅시다.

What do you think we're doing? 우리가 뭘 하고 있다고 보십니까?

Alternative Expressions

---

1 I've heard so much about you.

= *I've heard a lot about you.*
= *[Someone] has told me so much about you.*

---

2 I hope you don't mind my asking.

= *Do you mind if I ask~? May I ask~?*

---

3 What do you do in your free time?

= *What do you do in your spare time?*
= *What do you do for fun?*
= *What are your hobbies?*
= *Do you have any hobbies?*

---

4 Let me check my schedule.

= *Let me check my appointment book/planner/schedule.*
Let me get back to you.
Let me check my schedule and get back to you.

---

5 When should we meet?

= *What time were you thinking?*
= *What time is good for you?*

Focus on Pronunciation

영어의 철자 26개 가운데 모음의 역할을 하는 철자는 A, E, I, O, U 다섯 개입니다. 이 모음 철자는 강세를 받느냐, 혹은 받지 않느냐에 따라서 발음하는 방법이 달라집니다. 이를 잘 이해하고 기억하시면, 늘 우리가 궁금해하던, "도대체 왜 이 단어는 발음이 이래?"의 궁금증이 해결될 것입니다. 우선 강세를 받는 경우부터 살펴보겠습니다.

1. 강세를 받는 모음 a, e, i의 발음

모음이 강세를 받는 경우에는 다양하게 발음됩니다.

Vowel : a ❶ Short a [æ] : map, bag, hat, chat−chatting
❷ Long a [ei] : make, cake, hate−hating
❸ Long a [ei] : rain, paint, main
❹ Long a [ei] : May, play, say

Vowel : e ❶ Short e [e] : met, felt, Ken
❷ Long e [iː] : meet, feel, keen

Vowel : i ❶ Short i [i] : pin, kit, sit−sitting
❷ Long i [ai] : pine, kite, site, hike−hiking
❸ Long i [ai] : right, light, fight

본문 속 예문으로 살펴보고 발음해봅니다.

Actually, I'm in finance.
Michael gave me two tickets.

Real & Live

1. 잘해봐~ Go get her/him.

남녀가 서로 맘에 들어하거나 좋게 생각할 때 쓸 수 있는 표현입니다. get은 catch와
비슷한 의미로 볼 수 있는데요, "가서 그녀를, 혹은 그를 잡아!"라는 의미로 번역되지만
보통은 "서로 잘해보라"는 뜻으로 이 표현을 사용합니다. 가장 쉽게는 "Good luck!"을
사용하셔도 됩니다.

> A: Hey John, see that cute girl sitting there all by herself?
>   I'm going to try talking to her.
> B: It's about time you tried to get a date! Go get her!

2. 외모가 꽝이야. He has a face only a mother could love.

외모가 출중하지 못하고 못난 사람들
을 일컬어 이렇게 표현하는데, 직역
하면 '낳아준 엄마만이 사랑할 수
있는 외모야'라는 뜻이 됩니다.

반면에 한국어로 한때 "폭탄이
야"라는 표현이 '외모가 꽝이
다'라는 뜻으로 쓰인 적이 있습
니다. 재미있는 사실은 한국어를
그 대로 영 어 로 표 현 해 서,
"She's a bomb"나 "He's

bomb"라고 한다면, 의도한 것과는 반대로 "그녀는 너무 멋져" 혹은 "그는 너무 매력적이야"가 된다는 겁니다.

> A: Hey, do you think Charles is handsome?
> B: Well, no. He has a face that only a mother could love.
> But he has nice manners.

3. 나도 한때 잘 나갔는데. I used to be hot.

한창 잘 나가던 예전의 추억을 떠올리며 할 수 있는 말이죠. Used to라는 표현을 쓰게 되면 '이전에는, 옛날에는 ~했었다'라는 의미를 가지게 됩니다. 멋지다라는 hot을 이용해서 나도 한때는 멋졌다라고 해서 이런 표현을 쓸 수 있습니다. 남성들의 경우에는 "I used to be a player/a real ladies' man"이라는 표현을 쓰기도 합니다.

> A: Jenny, I heard that you used to be a player when you were
> single and younger.
> B: Yeah, but not anymore. I used to be hot, but after I got
> married, I lost my attractiveness.

Exercises

Choosing the Word

Fill in the blanks with the best possible expressions from the list. Pay attention to how the expressions are used grammatically. You may need to consider verb tenses, subject-verb agreement, etc.

favorite	fun	come here	used to	tell me
sounds	coincidence	Would you like	playing	love

Aaron   This is a really huge park. Do you (1)_____ often?

Hannah   Yes, quite a bit. How about you? Do you like the outdoors?

Aaron   Well, I (2)_____ . But not anymore. I prefer staying indoors now.

Hannah   Really! Then (3)_____ more about your other hobbies. I'd like to know more about you.

Aaron   Well, I really enjoy (4)_____ board games at home.

Hannah   Oh, I (5)_____ board games!

Aaron   Really? Of all the board games, what's your (6)_____ game?

Hannah   Let's see. I play a lot of chess, but Monopoly is probably the most (7)_____ for me.

Aaron   What a (8)_____ ! So we do have something in common after all!

Hannah   (9)_____ to play a game of Monopoly with some of my friends this weekend?

Aaron   Sure, that (10)_____ great!

Lesson 4

Going to the Performance

• After the performance

Alex Well, **what did you think** of the show?

Soyeong That was excellent! What about you?

Alex Yeah, I was impressed. **My favorite part** was the last scene.

Soyeong I agree. The acting and singing were really good.

Alex Especially the singing. The leading actress was amazing!

Soyeong Yes, she had a lovely voice. Michael must be proud. He really did a good job directing.

Alex Hey, why don't we go backstage and say hello to Michael?

Soyeong [*Laughing.*] Sure! That sounds like fun!

• Backstage

Michael Soyeong! Alex! Glad you could make it. So, what did you guys think?

Soyeong Wow! **We were both so impressed!** You're a famous director now!

Alex Yeah, **can I get your autograph?**

Michael [*Laughing.*] **Of course** you can! [*Signs autograph.*]

Key Patterns

1. I was _____.   I was impressed.
2. That sounds like _____.   That sounds like fun.
3. Why don't we _____?

   Why don't we go backstage and say hello to Michael?

1

I was _____. 저는 _____ 했어요.
I was impressed.

"impress something on someone" 무언가로 누군가를 감동시킨다는 표현의 수동태이며, "be impressed (upon/by)~"으로 무엇엔가 감명을 받았다는 뜻으로 사용합니다. 사람을 주어로 해서 사용할 수 있습니다.

I was impressed by her hard work.
그녀의 열심히 일하는 모습이 감동적이었습니다.
I was moved by their acting in the movie.
영화 속에서 그들의 연기를 보고 감동받았어요.

2

That sounds like _____. _____ 처럼 들려요.
That sounds like fun.

주어 + sound like + 명사 패턴으로 "(상대편이 말하는 것을 들어보니) ~인 것 같다"는 뜻으로, like 다음에 명사나 절이 옵니다.

You sound like your mom. 당신 꼭 어머님처럼 말하는구려.
It sounds like you've fallen in love. 너 사랑에 빠진 것처럼 들려.

주어 + Sound + 형용사의 경우라면 '주어가 ~한 것 같다'고 이해하시면 되죠.

Doesn't it sound a little strange? 좀 이상하게 들리지 않아요?
He sounds excited. 그 사람 흥분한 것처럼 들려요.
It sounds good. 좋아요.

3

Why don't we _____? 우리 _____ 할까요?
Why don't we go backstage and say hello to Michael?

"Why don't we/you~?"는 권유하거나 의견을 물을 때 가장 많이 사용하는 패턴입니다.

Why don't we go home and take a rest? 우리집에 가서 쉬는 게 어때?
Why don't you come over to my place? 우리집에 놀러 오실래요?

We/you 자리에 상대편 대신에 he/she/they가 오면 원래의 뜻대로 "왜 ~을 안하는 건가요?"라는 뜻이 됩니다. 주의하세요.

Why doesn't he go home? 왜 그 사람은 집에 안 간대요?
Why don't they do that work themselves? 그들은 왜 스스로들 안 할까요?

Alternative Expressions

1   What did you think~?
= *What is your opinion?*
= *What are your thoughts on~?*

2   My favorite part was ~ .
= *I really liked ~ the most.*
= *I loved ~ .*

3   We are both so impressed!
= *That was quite impressive.*
= *That was really great.*
= *That was really awesome.*
= *That was really wonderful.*

4   Can I get your autograph?
We need your signature* here.
Please sign here.
Your signature is required here.
   * Signatures are required for formal documents.
     Autographs are from celebrities or famous people.

5   Of course.
Absolutely. I'd be happy to [do that for you].
My pleasure!
Certainly!

Focus on Pronunciation

2. 강세를 받는 모음 o, u의 발음 &
강세를 받지 않는 a, e, i, o, u 애매모음

A, E, I, O, U 모음이 강세를 받는 경우에는 각기 다양한 방법으로 발음됩니다. 그러나 이 모음 철자 다섯 개가 강세를 받지 않는 경우 대부분은 /ə/로 발음됩니다.

Vowel : o　❶ Short o [ɔ] : hot, mop, pot
　　　　　　　❷ Long o [u] : book, cook, foot
　　　　　　　❸ Long o [ou] : snow, window, low

Vowel : u　❶ Short u [ʌ] : bug, sun, run-running
　　　　　　　❷ Long u [ju] : sure, tune, mule

　Schwa(애매모음) [ə] : 모음들이 강세를 받지 않을 때

　　ex) **cycle vs. bicycle**

Cycle은 강세를 받으므로 y를 [ai]로 발음하지만, bicycle은 강세가 i에 있으므로 y는 [ə]로 발음합니다.

본문 속 예문을 통해 모음 발음이 어떻게 다른지 살펴보세요.

　My favorite part was the last scene. ➔ a 중심
　We were both so impressed! ➔ o 중심
　Sure! That sounds like fun! ➔ u 중심

1. 내가 쏠게. I'll get this.

"제가 쏠께요!"라는 표현을 영어로 알아봅시다. Get 동사를 사용해서 "I'll get this"나 "I'll get the bill"이라고 하면 '자신이 그걸/계산서를 집는다' 는 뜻으로 지불하겠다는 의사가 있다는 뜻으로 해석됩니다. 같은 의미의 다른 표현으로는 "It's on me"나 "My treat"을 사용하기도 합니다.

A: Wow, the bill for our meal is expensive.
B: Don't worry. I'll get this. I just got a raise at work.

2. 꽝이야 vs. 대박이야! That's terrible. vs. That rocks!

절망적이고 안좋은 상황을 나타내는 표현은 terrible, awful과 같은 형용사를 이용해서 표현하시면 됩니다. 이와 반대되는 의미로 좋은 상황에서는 "That rocks!"라고 하는데요, 영어로 rock은 '돌, 혹은 구르다'는 뜻에서 이제 '멋지다, 끝내준다, 죽이게 좋다'라는 표현으로도 자연스럽게 사용됩니다.

우선 매우 구어적인 표현이라는 점을 짚고 넘어가도록 하겠습니다. 친구들이나 친한 사람들 사이에서 한국어로 "진짜 죽음이야~" 혹은 "~쩐다~쩔어"라는 표현을 사용할 때 그 의미를 영어 단어 'rock'을 사용해서 표현해보세요. 생생하게 살아 있는 표현으로 외치는 겁니다. "이 영어회화 과목 진짜, 킹왕짱!"이라고 표현하려면 말 그대로 "You know what, this class rocks!"라고 하시면 되겠죠?

A: How do you like your new car?
B: It rocks! I love it.

3. 음악에 일가견이 있어. You have good taste in music.

어떤 한 분야에 조예가 깊은 사람을 일컬어 일가견이 있다고 하는데요, 일가견은 영어로 "good taste"라고 합니다. 이는 좋은 심미안을 가졌다는 의미로 해석할 수 있습니다. 그리고 어떤 분야인지를 말해줄 때에는 'in'이라는 전치사를 이용해서 말한다는 것도 체크해두세요!

A: Would you like to listen to my MP3?
B: This sounds great. You have good taste in music.

Exercises

• Crossword Puzzle

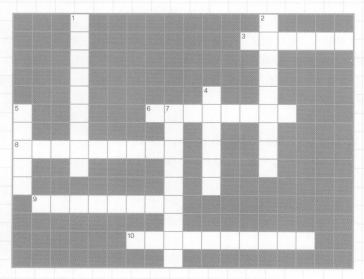

Down

1. If something _____ you, it affected you favorably
2. A section of the theater which refers to the area behind the stage
4. An adjective that describes being filled with delight
5. In a play, film, or book, this is the place where the action occurs
7. The signature of someone famous which is specially written for a fan

Across

3. Someone or something that is very well known
6. Something that you like the most
8. Outstanding, good, great, fine, cool
9. Person who decides how a play will appear on stage or screen and who tells the actors and technical staff what to do
10. An adverb that emphasizes a special or particular quality

Culture Corner

• Football

American football is one of the most popular team sports in the United States and Canada. Although the game evolved from rugby and soccer in the late 19th and early 20th centuries, American football differs in rules, strategy, equipment and scoring. Every year, usually in January or February, the National Football League (NFL) holds the Super Bowl championship. This game is held on a Sunday. It

is the most watched television event in the United States. It has become so popular that some people consider "Superbowl Sunday" to be a minor national holiday.

The game itself is normally played on a grass field that is 100 yards long. The goal is to reach the far end of the field, called the "end zone," to score points. When one team carries or passes the ball into the end zone, it is called a "touchdown" or "TD" for short. Each touchdown is worth six points; a scoring team can earn one extra point with a kick that goes between the goal posts.

One team has eleven players with possession of the ball. This is called the "offense." They attempt to score by advancing the ball to the end zone. The other team also has eleven players. They are called the "defense." Their job is to block or prevent the team from advancing and scoring. If the offense fails to score after four attempts, then the offensive and defensive teams switch roles. Sometimes, the defensive team will gain possession of the ball by catching a pass intended for the offense. This is called an "interception." Or sometimes the offense will drop the ball while carrying it. This is called a "fumble."

The quarterback position is perhaps the most important position on the offensive team. He is responsible for passing, throwing and sometimes carrying the ball himself into the end zone to score points. However, football is a team sport and requires a great deal of cooperation in order to win. Some observers consider American football to be a symbol of American culture and values.

- **What term describes when a team scores six points in the end zone?**

- **What is perhaps the most important position on the offensive team?**

Theme III

Working Life

In Theme III, we take a closer look at the work life of Alex, who works in finance. After confirming a business meeting with Liz, an overseas business executive who will be visiting Seoul, Alex then accompanies Liz as she shops for her family in the famous Insadong area. At the end of the section, the scene shift to examine one of the consequences of after–work drinking. Alex is hungover from too many drinks. As it turns out, Michael and Matthew, Jennifer's boyfriend, are also hungover.

Confirming the Meeting

Mary	Good morning, this is Smithfield Company. How may I help you?
Alex	Hi, **this is Alex Choi from Korea calling** for Ms. Liz Chapman.
Mary	**I'm sorry, Ms. Chapman isn't in the office at the moment. May I take a message?**
Alex	I was just calling because I would like to talk about her visit to Seoul next week. When do you expect her to return to the office?
Mary	She should be back within the hour.
Alex	OK, then please have her call me back when she returns.
Mary	Certainly. **And may I have your last name again?**
Alex	It's Choi. C-h-o-i.
Mary	Thank you, Mr. Choi. I'll make sure she gets your message.

* * * *

Alex's Secretary	This is Financial Korea Investments. May I help you?
Liz Chapman	Hi. This is Liz Chapman. I'm calling for Mr. Choi.
Secretary	**One moment please. I'll put you through.**
Alex	Hi, Liz! Nice to hear from you. So you got my message?
Liz	Hi, Alex! Yes, and I'm looking forward to seeing you next week in Seoul. We have a lot of exciting ventures to talk about.

Key Patterns

1. I would like to _____.
   I would like to talk about her visit to Seoul next week.

2. We have a lot of _____.
   We have a lot of exciting ventures to talk about.

3. When *do you expect* ( ) to _____?
   When *do you expect* her **to** return to the office?

1

I would like to _____.

저는 _____ 하고 싶습니다.

I would like to talk about her visit to Seoul next week.

I would like to + 동사는 "~하고 싶다"는 정중한 표현으로 특히 성인 화자들의 경우 I want to보다 회화는 물론 작문에서도 활용도가 높으니 잘 익혀두세요.

I would like to ask you whether you are available this afternoon.
오늘 오후에 시간이 되는지 여쭙고 싶은데요.

Would like to는 무언가를 권하거나 의향을 물어볼 때도 유용합니다. 특히 음식을 권할 때 "(일반적으로) 무엇을 좋아하세요"의 Do you like~?보다는 "지금 이 순간 원하는 것/음식이 무엇입니까?", "Would you like~?"가 훨씬 적절한 것 이해하시죠?

Would you like to try this red dress on?
붉은 원피스 입어보실래요?

Would you like another coffee?
커피 한 잔 더 할래?

2

We have a lot of _____.

우리는 _____ 할 것이 많아요.

We have a lot of exciting ventures to talk about.

"We have + 명사" 입니다. '~ 이 많다' 는 뜻이죠.

We have many things common.

우리는 공통점이 많군요.

We have + 명사 + 동사는 '~할 것이 많다' 는 뜻이 됩니다.

We have many wonderful people to work with.

우리는 함께 일할 수 있는 좋은 사람들이 많이 있습니다.

When do you expect (   ) to _____?

언제 _____ 할 것 같아요?

When do you expect her to return to the office?

When do you expect (   ) + 동사는 "언제 ~할 것 같아요?"라고 일을 언제 할 예정인지, 혹은 도착과 출발 시간이 어떻게 되는지 물어보는 표현으로 매우 유용합니다.

When do you expect to take the flight?
당신은 언제 비행기를 타실 예정인가요?

When do you expect to be hired?
언제쯤 취직될 것 같으세요?

When do you expect him to stop smoking?
그 사람은 언제쯤 담배를 끊을까요?

Alternative Expressions

1 This is Alex Choi from Korea calling for~.

I'd like to speak with [name].

This is [name] calling from [company]. May I speak with [name], please?

2 I'm sorry, Ms. Chapman isn't in the office at the moment.

He/she has stepped out of the office for a moment.

He's not in [the office] at the moment.

She stepped out for a moment.

She is out of the office for the day.

She is unavailable at the moment.

She is away on business and will be back on [date].

3 May I take a message?

= May I say who is calling?

= Would you like to leave a message on his voicemail?

4 May I have your last name again?

= How do you spell that, sir?

= May I have the spelling of your last name?

5 One moment please. I'll put you through.

= Please hold while I transfer you [to his voicemail].

= Certainly, Mr. Jones. One moment while I transfer you.

= One moment, please. I will transfer you.

Focus on Pronunciation

● Part 3. 자 음

모음 사이의 x의 발음

X의 발음은 강세의 위치에 따라 다르게 발음합니다. 강세가 앞의 모음에 오면 [ks]로 발음하고 강세가 뒤의 모음에 오면 [gz]로 발음합니다. 같은 철자의 발음이 달라지는 것을 확인하시기 전에, 우선 각 단어를 강세를 넣어서 발음해보세요. 강세가 어디에 있는지, 각 쌍을 이룬 두 단어의 강세가 달라지는 것이 입에서 느껴지시나요? 그 다음 발음 기호에 맞추어서 정확히 발음해봅니다.

[ks]	[gz]
execute	executive
luxury	luxurious
exit	exist

본문 속 예문을 통해 단어의 강세는 어디에 있으며, 어떻게 발음되는지 확인해보십시오.

I'm looking forward to seeing you next week in Seoul.
We have a lot of exciting ventures to talk about.

Real & Live

1. 그 프로젝트 잘 되어가나요? How are you doing on that project?

우리는 안부인사로 How are you doing?을 자주 사용합니다. 바로 그 뒤에 on this /that project만 덧붙여서, 유용한 표현을 만들었습니다. 그 계획안이 잘 진행되고 있는지 묻는 표현이죠. 아예 주어를 계획으로 가져가는 표현으로 "How is this project going?"도 물론 가능합니다.

> A: Mr. Johnson, how are you doing on that project?
> B: The project is going very well, sir. It should be completed by the end of the week.

2. (일을) 잘 처리하고 있습니다. It's in good hands.

'제 손, 특히 업무를 잘 수행하는 손 안에 있습니다'라는 뜻으로 '그것만큼은 제가 최고죠'라고 해석할 수 있겠습니다. 최고가 관리하고 있다, 그러니까 '일이나 계획들이 잘 처리되고 있다, 안심하셔도 된다'는 표현이 됩니다. 다른 표현들을 알아볼까요?

> Don't worry. I didn't drop the ball.

'걱정하지 마세요, 제가 그 공 안 떨어뜨렸잖아요'입니다. 일을 손에 쥐고 있는 공에 비유한 것으로, 바닥에 떨어뜨리지 않고, 잘 들고 있다, 공이 제자리에 있다, 결국 업무가 아무런 무리 없이 잘 진행되고 있다는 뜻으로 해석하시면 됩니다.

> A: I'm really nervous about my surgery, Nurse.

B: Don't worry, Mr. Jones. You're in good hands. Dr. Lee is the
best surgeon in the city.

3. 나 요즘 너무 바빠요. I have a full plate.

물론 쉽게는 "I'm really busy"나 "I'm so packed"라고 하면 바쁘다는 표현이 됩니
다. 그러나 Real & Live를 통해 좀 더 생생한 구어적 표현을 익혀보지요. plate는 음식
을 담고 있는 접시라는 뜻입니다. 그럼 왜 '먹을 것이 가득한 접시를 갖고 있다'는 표현
이 '너무 바쁘다'가 됐을까요? 한 접시에 이것 저것 잔뜩 올려져 있고, 여러분들은 그
접시 위에 놓여 있는 다양한 음식을 먹어야 해요. 그래요, 그러니까 결국 바쁘다는 겁니
다. 얼만큼? 아주 많이. "I have a full plate"라는 표현 잘 익혀두세요. 유용하게 사용
하실 수 있을 겁니다.

A: Mary, do you think you can babysit my son tomorrow night?
B: I'm sorry Elizabeth, but I have a full plate tomorrow night.
Maybe some other time.

Exercises

Error Correction

Find the errors and make corrections.

1. What's Seoul?

2. I was impress.

3. Thanks for come.

4. I'm so happy to you.

5. You're such good girl.

6. Have I take a message?

7. What do you think for movies?

8. Let's all getting together for lunch.

9. Why do we going backstage and saying hello to Michael?

10. I would like to telling touch base about her visit in Seoul.

Shopping

Liz	Wonderful! What's this place called?
Alex	This is Insadong. It's a traditional Korean marketplace. You can get something for your children here. It's a great place to shop for souvenirs, but it's quite crowded!
Liz	Yes, it's really busy. Oh, gorgeous! What are these?
Alex	Those are traditional Korean dolls.
Liz	Lovely. Absolutely lovely. They're so **delicate and colorful.**
Shopkeeper	**Can I help you?**
Alex	We're just looking, thank you.
Shopkeeper	**If you need anything, just let me know.**
Liz	What are these?
Alex	These are traditional Korean cookies and candy. How much are these?
Shopkeeper	3,000 won.
Liz	Delightful! I'll take one of each, please.

Key Patterns

1. I'll take _____. I'll **take** one of each, please.

2. It's quite _____. It's **quite** crowded.

3. How much _____? **How much** are these?

1

I'll take _____.

저는 _____ 로 할게요.

I'll take one of each, please.

I'll+ 동사는 '내가 ~해 보겠다'는 뜻으로, 자신의 결심이나 생각, 앞으로 행하게 될 행동을 알려줍니다. 특히 I'll be~, I'll see~, I'll tell~, I'll take~ 등이 자주 사용되고, 이때 take는 가지다는 뜻으로 유추하시면 됩니다.

I'll take + 명사 패턴을 익혀두시고, 교통수단을 이야기할 때에도 유용하다는 점을 기억하세요.

I'll take it. 그걸로 하겠어요.
I'll take a shower first. 샤워부터 할래요.
I'll take the subway. 지하철 타지요, 뭐.

2

It's quite _____.

꽤 _____ 하군요.

It's quite crowded.

군중이라는 명사 crowd에서 crowded라는 '사람들로 꽉 찬'이라는 형용사가 나왔습니다. 출퇴근 시간의 대중교통을 생각하거나, 인파로 가득한 거리를 상상해보세요. pack도 포장하다는 뜻으로만 알기 쉬운데, 어떤 장소로 사람들이 모여들어 채운다는 뜻이 있습니다.

Seoul is a crowded city of 15 million.   서울 인구는 1천5백만 명이에요.
It's quite packed.   사람들로 붐비네요.
Thousands of people packed into the stadium.

수천 명의 사람들이 운동장을 꽉 채우고 있습니다.

How much _____?

_____ 는 얼마입니까?

How much are these?

A. How much _____?는 가격을 물어볼 때 가장 유용하죠. 셀 수 없는 것에 사용하고 How much + 동사? 혹은 How much + 셀 수 없는 명사 + 동사구가 주로 사용됩니다.

How much do you want? 얼마나 필요하십니까?

How much money have you made from your record?

그 음반으로 얼마나 버셨습니까?

How much time and effort did you put into making this?

이 일을 이루시기 위해 얼마나 많은 시간과 노력을 들이셨나요?

B. How much does it cost _____?도 가격에 대한 표현으로 유용하니까, 좀 더 익혀보죠.

How much does it cost to ride the subway?

지하철 요금이 얼마예요?

How much does it cost for a coffee?

커피 한 잔에 얼마지?

Alternative Expressions

---

1   *It can get really crowded.*
It's really packed!
It's jampacked with people.
It can get really hectic.

---

2   Delicate and colorful.

Delightful!	*Wonderful!*	*Splendid!*	*Terrific!*
Awesome!	*Cool!*	*Great!*	*Sweet!*

---

3   Can I help you?
= *Is there anything I can help you with today?*
= *May I help you find something?*

---

4   If you need anything, just let me know.
= *Please let me know if I can be of any assistance.*

---

5   How much are these?
= *What is the price on these?*
= *How much do these go for?*

Focus on Pronunciation

구개음화

자음 /t, d, s, z/가 강세를 받지 않는 모음 /i/ 또는 /y/ 앞에 있는 경우 / tʃ, dʒ, ʃ, ʒ /로 발음합니다.

t + y(i) = tʃ / ㅌ+ 이 = 같이 [가치]

Nice to meet you.
I got you.

d + y(i) = dʒ / ㄷ + 이 = 굳이 [구지]

Would you mind leaving?
Did you eat?

s + y(i) = ʃ

I miss you so much.

/ʒ/

what version are your using?
What's your vision for this year?

Real & Live

1. 유행이야. It's in.

최신 유행하고 있는 것을 가리킬 때 in이라고 합니다. 반대로 out을 쓰면 유행이 지나갔다는 것을 말합니다. 가장 최근의 것이라고 해서 "the latest thing"이라는 표현도 사용할 수 있고 구어적인 표현으로는 가장 잘 쓰이는 형용사 "hot"을 이용해서 표현하셔도 좋습니다.

> It's the latest thing.
> It's trendy these days.
> It's really hot.

A: Linda, I love your new purse!
B: Yes, it's in these days. Everyone has one.

2. 괜찮은 가격이네. What a deal!

판매 가격에 대해 만족을 나타내는 표현으로 사용됩니다. 여기서 deal은 상당량, 즉 많은 양을 뜻하며 가격에 비해 양이 많아 싸다고 생각되는 상품들을 일컬어 '가격이 괜찮다'라고 표현할 수 있습니다. 다른 표현으로는 "It's a steal"을 사용할 수 있습니다. steal은 '도둑질, 훔친 물건'을 뜻하는데 여기서는 훔친 물건처럼 '거의 공짜로 얻은 물건이나 다름없다'는 의미가 되어 '매우 저렴하다/무척 싸다'는 뜻이 됩니다.

A: Can you believe that I bought this purse for 50 percent off?
   It was such a steal!
B: What a deal! You're really fortunate.

3. 반드시 사야 할 물건이야! It's a must-have (item).

쇼핑에 관심이 많은 분들이라면 머스트 해브 아이템이라는 표현을 많이 들어보셨을 거에요. '반드시 사야 할 물건'이라는 표현인데 우리나라에서도 영어 표현을 그대로 가져다 쓰고 이제는 거의 고유명사화된 것 같습니다. 이 표현 외에도 "It's something you can't do without"이라는 표현이 있는데요 '그것 없이 아무것도 할 수 없다'라는 의미로 반드시 필요하다는 걸 강조해주는 말이겠죠? 이제부터 쇼핑할 때 "이건 반드시 사야해!"라고 말해주고 싶을 때 외쳐주세요!

A: Jason, look at this ad for a new computer web camera.
  It's a must-have item.
B: Yeah, I heard that you can't do without it for communication
  these days. I'm going to buy one right away.

Exercises

• Select the Appropriate Word

1. Can I get your _____? (to someone famous)
    a. autograph   b. signature

2. What's this place _____?
    a. call   b. called

3. Lovely. Absolutely _____!
    a. terrible   b. gorgeous

4. What do you think about _____?
    a. go to a movie   b. going to a movie

5. They are so _____ and _____.
    a. delicate, sweet   b. delicious, tasteless

6. This is Alex from Korea _____ for Liz.
    a. to call   b. calling

7. We have a lot of _____ ventures to talk about.
    a. exciting   b. excite

Hangover

Soyeong Why do you look so sick?

Alex Is it that obvious? I had a bit too much to drink after work last night, I guess.

Michael You too? Matthew and I went bar hopping last night. I'm hungover from too many **mixed drinks.**

Matthew Yeah, I drank like a fish. Big mistake. **Do you like to drink?**

Soyeong Me? Oh no. I can't hold my liquor very well.

Alex I can't handle mixed drinks. They're too strong for me. I usually stick with beer.

Michael Yeah, if I drink too much, I wake up the next morning feeling terrible. Did you pass out last night?

Alex No. Thank God. I was able to eat some soup this morning. It helped settle my stomach.

Soyeong If your stomach is OK, drinking lots of fluids can help you feel better, too.

Matthew Yes, I've heard of that. I either have to cut down on my drinking or not drink at all. **It makes me feel sick all the time.**

Soyeong That's a good idea!

Key Patterns

1. I can't _____.
   I can't hold my liquor very much.
2. Either A or B _____.
   I **either** have to cut down on my drinking or not drink at all.
3. Why *do* you _____?
   Why *do* **you** look so sick?

1

I can't _____. 나는 _____ 할 수 없어요.

I can't hold my liquor very well.

'할 수 있다'는 I can, '할 수 없다'는 I can't 입니다. 도저히 자신의 능력으로 행할
수 없는 일에 대한 표현으로 I can't + 동사 패턴을 사용하세요. 쉽죠?

I can't do this any more. 더 이상은 할 수 없어요.
I can't help it. 저도 어쩔 수가 없어요.

A. I can't stand _____. _____ 을 참을 수 없다.

조금 다른 표현으로는 stand 뒤에 명사나 to 동사가 옵니다.

I can't stand to be all alone.
혼자 있는 건 정말 너무 힘들어.
I can't stand that TV drama.
저는 그 텔레비전 드라마는 볼 수가 없어요.

68

2

Either A or B. A거나 B거나.

I either have to cut down on my drinking or not drink at all.

Either은 '둘 중 하나'라는 뜻
으로, 주로 or가 함께 오지요. Either
A or B 즉, 'A거나 B거나'라는 표현
으로 많이 외웁니다. 가장 간단하게는
A 혹은 B에 명사를 넣습니다.

I would like to have either pizza or bibimbap for lunch.
점심으로 피자나 비빔밥 먹을래요.
He's either an angel or a devil. 그는 천사거나 혹은 악마야.

그 외 본문처럼 either A or B에서 A와 B 위치에 동사나 형용사가 올 수도 있고, 부
정문 제일 끝에, too 대신 either를 사용해서, '~도 역시'라는 뜻을 나타내기도 합
니다. 가장 중요한 것은 A와 B가 동일한 품사로 댓구를 이룬다는 사실입니다. 꼭 기
억하세요!

He is either telling a lie or making an excuse.
그는 지금 거짓말을 하고 있거나 변명을 대고 있어.
All men are created equal : either you believe it or you don't.
당신이 믿든 믿지 않든, 모든 인간은 평등하게 태어났습니다.

3

Why do you _____?

왜 _____ 하는 거죠?

Why do you look so sick?

why do you + 동사 ?는 이유를 묻는 의문문입니다.

Why do you ask me again?

저한테 다시 묻는 이유가 뭐예요?

Why do you think I don't listen to you?

너는 내가 왜 네 말을 듣지 않는다고 생각하는 건데?

A. 주어 + look + 형용사 패턴도 Why 의문문 못지않게 중요합니다. Look 다음 형용사가 주어를 수식하는 보어로, "~처럼 보이다"라는 의미를 갖습니다.

You look impressed.

너 감동받았구나.

They look great together.

그들은 꽤 잘 어울려요.

이 문장에 도전해보실래요?

Green looks really great on you.

녹색이 참 잘 어울리시네요.

Alternative Expressions

1   Why do you look so sick?

= *You don't look so hot.*

= *Are you okay?*

= *You don't look so great.*

= *You look tired.*

= *Are you feeling all right?*

2   **mixed drink**: a drink where two or more drinks are mixed together

(Examples)

Screwdriver: vodka and orange juice

Bloody Mary: vodka and tomato juice

Gin & Tonic: gin with tonic water

3   Do you like to drink?

= *Do you drink?*

= *Can you drink a lot?*

= *Can he handle his liquor [well]?*

     teetotaler: a person who does not drink alcohol at all

4

Q: Do you like to drink?

A: Responses

- *I enjoy a beer/scotch/cocktail/glass of wine every now and then.*
- *I am an occasional drinker.*
- *He/She is a heavy drinker.*
- *He doesn't know how to handle his liquor.*
- *He's an alcoholic.*
- *He's a mean/nasty drunk.*
- *He has a drinking problem.*
- *He gets ugly when he drinks.*

5

It makes me feel sick all the time.

I feel terrible/horrible/sick/nauseous.

I feel like I'm going to throw up/vomit/barf.

= I think I'm going to be sick.

Focus on Pronunciation

Th의 발음

th의 발음은 일반적으로 /θ/로 하지만, 모음과 모음 사이에 th가 오는 경우와 th 다음에 e가 와서 th+e의 형태로 맨앞에 오는 경우 th는 /ð/로 발음합니다.

일반적인 경우: ba**th**, brea**th**, **th**in /θ/
모음 사이에 th가 오는 경우: ba**th**e, brea**th**e, wea**th**er /ð/
Th 다음에 e가 오는 경우: **th**ey, **th**ere, **th**em /ð/

본문 속 예문에서는 Matthew와 they라는 단어에서 이 발음을 찾아볼 수 있습니다.

Ma**tth**ew and I went bar hopping last night.   /θ/
They are too strong for me.   /ð/

Real & Live

1. 건배! Cheers!

여럿이 모인 술자리에서 빠짐없이 등장하는 말이죠? 모두 잔을 높이 들고서 외치는 이 말을 영어로 해볼까요? 가장 간단하고 쓰기 쉬운 표현이 "Cheers!"라면 "위하여!"라고 외칠 땐 "To your health!"라고 하세요. 직역하면 '건강을 위하여'입니다만, health 대신에 다른 단어를 사용하셔도 좋습니다. 무언가를 위해서 건배를 할 때 "To your _____!"라고 외치세요!

> A: Hey everybody, let's drink!
> B: Cheers! To your health!

2. 나 오바이트 했어. I threw up what I ate.

우리나라에서 오바이트라는 말은 '토하다'라는 의미로 사용되고 있는데 이는 대표적인 콩글리쉬 표현입니다. 오바이트는 영어 overeat에서 나온 표현으로 overeat의 원래 영어 뜻은 '과식하다'입니다. 아마도 무리하게 과식한 사람들이 주로 하는 행위에서 비롯된 표현이 아닐까 싶은데요, 우리가 흔히 말하는 '토하다'에 해당하는 영어 표현은 throw up이라는 동사입니다.

> A: I don't feel so good. I think I drank too much beer last night.
> B: Me too. I even threw up everything I ate.

74

3. 속 쓰려. My stomach is killing me.

술 마신 다음날 이런 경험이 있으신가요? 속이 너무 아파 힘들 때 하는 말로 영어에서는 '내 위가 날 죽이고 있어'라고 표현합니다. 위가 좋지 않아 그 고통이 죽을 만큼 힘들다고 말하는 거죠.

이 표현을 응용해서 무언가 너무 힘든 일이 있을 때 "Something is killing me"라고 하실 수 있습니다. 예를 들어 시험 때문에 너무 힘들다고 말하고 싶을 때 "The test is killing me"라고 하는 겁니다. 이런 표현은 알아두시면 좋지만 쓸 일이 많지 않아야겠죠?

A: John, are you okay? You don't look so well.
B: It's this terrible headache. My head is killing me!

Exercises

Collocation Match Up

Collocations are special combinations of words that can be idioms or other phrases and expressions. Find collocations from Lessons 1 to 7 by matching the words from Column A with words in Column B.

A.

1. look _____ sure
2. thanks _____ down on
3. sound _____ my liquor
4. take _____ with
5. make _____ so cute
6. put _____ through
7. look _____ forward to ~ing
8. hold _____ like fun
9. stick _____ a message
10. cut _____ for ~ing

B.

Culture Corner

• American Currency

American money consists of bills and coins. Paper money, known as bills, can be called "cash," "bills," or simply by its most basic unit, "dollars." The $1 dollar bill is also known as a "buck" and can be used as a unit for counting (for example, "twenty bucks" = $20).

Here are the famous historical figures printed on each bill:

$1   George Washington, the 1st president of America
$2   Thomas Jefferson, the 3rd president of America
$5   Abraham Lincoln, the 16th president of America
$10   Alexander Hamilton, the 1st US Secretary of the Treasury
$20   Andrew Jackson, the 7th president of America
$50   Ulysses S. Grant, the 18th president of America
$100   Benjamin Franklin, one of the Founding Fathers of America

American coin denominations are:

The "penny"or one cent. It features a portrait of President Abraham Lincoln.

The "nickel" or five cents. It features a portrait of President Thomas Jefferson.

The "dime" or ten cents. It features a portrait of President Franklin D. Roosevelt.

The "quarter" or 25 cents. It features a portrait of President George Washington.

The "half−dollar" or "50−cent piece." It features a portrait of President John F. Kennedy.

In addition, there are three different one dollar coins: the "Susan B. Anthony," named after a famous women's rights leader, the "Sacagawea," the name of a famous Native American woman; and the "Gold dollar" featuring the Statue of Liberty.

Cost(s) a pretty penny
Meaning: To be very expensive
Example: "That new bicycle will cost you a pretty penny."

A penny for your thoughts.
Meaning: A person is lost in his or her thoughts; a person is daydreaming
Example: "Hey! A penny for your thoughts! What are you thinking about?"

A day late and a dollar short
Meaning: This means that one is too late, ill−prepared and/or insufficient to meet the needs of something.
Example: "I'm sorry, but I cannot accept your apology and take you back since I now have a new boyfriend. Seems like you are a day late and a dollar short."

Bang for the buck

Meaning: To get a very good value on something for the money that was paid

Example: (A) "Not only does the restaurant serve you large portions, you also get free refills and free parking validation."

(B) "Wow! You really get more bang for your buck at this restaurant!"

Big bucks

Meaning: A very large amount of money

Example: "My friend is now making big bucks by working at that successful internet company."

Make a quick/fast buck

Meaning: To make money very quickly, often through somewhat tricky or slightly illegal means

Example: "Well, he's now in jail because he thought he could make a fast buck off all those poor investors."

● **Who is on the five‒dollar bill?**

● **It is sometimes difficult to hear the difference between "fifty" (50) and "fifteen" (15). Using English words, try pronouncing "fifty cents" and "fifteen cents."**

Studying

In Theme IV, the focus shifts from the workplace to the classroom. Here, we are introduced to Stella, an English conversation teacher. Soyeong and her classmates learn about pronunciation difficulties and tips on how to study English on their own.

Pronunciation Problems!

Ben	Hey, Soyeong. What are you eating?
Soyeong	Stella brought some snacks for the class.
Ben	**Excuse me? What did you say?**
Soyeong	"Snacks." Why do you ask?
Ben	Uh, wait a minute. **I think I'm confused.** What does "snakes" mean?
Soyeong	**Snacks**-it's like food you eat between meals such as crackers, chips, cookies and stuff like that.
Ben	Oh! Snacks! I thought you said "snakes!" It sounds confusing sometimes! It's difficult to tell the difference in pronunciation!
Stella	**What are you guys laughing about?**
Soyoung	Ben thought I said "snakes" instead of "snacks."
Stella	Yes, pronunciation can be very confusing.
Ben	Sometimes it's so hard to tell the difference between the meaning and pronunciation of words!
Stella	Well, today **we'll discuss how** to improve pronunciation in our class.

Key Patterns

1. I said _____.
   Ben thought I **said** "snakes" instead of "snacks."

2. It's difficult to _____.
   It's difficult to tell the difference in pronunciation!

3. What are you _____ ?   **What are you** eating?

1

I said _____.   나는 _____ 라고 말했어요.

Ben thought I said "snakes" instead of "snacks."

Say의 동사 과거형 said 대신에 아예 다른 동사의 과거형을 넣어서 문장들을 만들어봅시
다. I + 동사 과거형을 사용한 문장입니다. 당연히 과거에 일어난 일을 지금 설명하고 있는
상황이 되겠지요.

I told you that he didn't like Ashley.
그가 애쉴리를 좋아하지 않는다고 내가 이미 너한테 말했잖아.

I couldn't believe what you said about him.
당신이 그에 대해서 이야기한 것들을 내가 믿을 수 없어요.

2

It's difficult to _____.

_____ 하는 것은 어렵습니다.

It's difficult to tell the difference
in pronunciation!

84

It's difficult to _____ 에 동사를 넣어서 다양한 표현을 만들어보겠습니다.

It's difficult to learn Russian. 러시아어는 배우기가 어렵네요.
It's difficult to do many things at the same time.
동시에 여러 가지 일을 하는 것은 쉽지 않아요.

A. It's + 형용사 + to 동사형 문장으로 '~하는 것은 ~하다' 라는 구문으로 이 또한 활용도 높은 유용한 패턴이니 꼭 외워두세요. 영어는 사물을 주어로 하는 문장을 다양하게 사용한답니다.

It's very common to share housework together as a couple.
부부가 가사일을 분담하는 것은 매우 자연스러운 일이죠.
It's so hard to say goodbye to yesterday.
과거에 안녕을 고하는 것이 참 어렵군요.

3

What are you _____?
당신은 무엇을 _____ 있어요?
What are you eating?

What be 동사+주어+동사 진행형 문장입니다. 도대체 무엇을 하고 있냐는 거겠죠.

What are you thinking?
도대체 무슨 생각을 하고 있는 거예요?
What are you doing at the library?
당신은 도서관에서 뭘 하고 있어요?
What are you guys laughing about?
무엇 때문에 여러분들은 그렇게들 웃고 있어요?

Alternative Expressions

1 Excuse me? What did you say?

= *I'm sorry, could you repeat that?*

= *I'm sorry, I couldn't hear what you were saying.*

= *I'm sorry, I didn't catch that.*

= *I didn't catch what you just said.*

= *I didn't catch that last part.*

= *I'm sorry, I missed that last part.*

2 I think I'm confused.

= *I'm not sure I understand.*

= *I'm not sure I get it.*

= *Could you go over that one more time?*

= *I'm not sure I'm clear on this.*

= *Let me get this straight.*

3 Other words for "snacks":

Informal: munchies or fingerfood

Formal: *hors d'oevres or appetizers*

4 What are you guys langhing about?

= *What's so funny?*

= *Let me in on the joke!*

5 We'll discuss how~

= *We'll talk about that [in more detail].*

= *We'll go through that more closely.*

= *We'll go through how to improve an English pronunciation.*

Focus on Pronunciation

1. 일반 동사의 3인칭 현재형 −s 의 발음

단어가 유성음으로 끝나면 /z/로 발음하고, 무성음으로 끝나면 /s/로 발음합니다.

Cleans , needs /z/
looks, walks /s/
kisses, boxes /iz/

단 t로 끝나면 /ch/로 발음하며, 단어가 s, z, sh, x, ch로 끝나면 단어 끝에 es 가 오면서 /iz/로 발음합니다.

Hits, fits /ch/
Classes, boxes, /iz/

본문 속 예문에서 살펴보면, '～처럼 들린다'는 동사 sound 다음에 3인칭 현재 를 나타내기 위해 s가 붙었습니다. 어떻게 발음되는지 확인하셨어요?

It sounds confusing sometimes!

1. 뭐가 뭔지 모르겠어. I (just) don't get it.

아주 유용한 동사, get이 다시 등장합니다. Get이라는 동사가 '파악하다'라는 뜻이 있거든요. "I just don't get it. 그런데 도무지 파악이 안 되는군, 아휴, 이해가 안 가"라고 하는 것이 "I don't understand it. 저는 잘 이해가 가지 않는군요" 하는 표현과 뜻은 같지만 조금 더 구어적인 느낌이 나는 것, 느끼시지요?

같은 맥락으로, 물론 "I just don't understand"라고 해도 뜻은 통합니다만 "I just don't get it"이라고 하면 구어적인 느낌이 생생히 난다고 할 수 있겠습니다.

이밖에 다른 표현들은 다음과 같습니다.

> I'm lost.
> It went over my head.

A: Today's class was hard. I really tried to pay attention, but I couldn't understand what the teacher was saying.
B: Me too. It went over my head. I just don't get it.

2. 감 잡았어. I get it.

이해가 안 가는 경우 get 동사를 사용했지요? 이번에는 '이해했어요'라는 표현을 살펴보겠습니다. get 동사를 다시 사용하시면 되고 지금 이해를 하는지, 과거에 이해를 했는지에 따라 동사형 시제를 바꿔보시면 좋겠습니다. "Oh, I get it." 혹은 "I got it, I got it!" 쉬우면서도, 구어적이고, 활용도도 높으니 꼭 기억하시기 바랍니다. Did you get it?

A: Hey! If you do that again, I won't be your friend anymore.
   Do you understand me?
B: Yeah, I get it, I get it. I promise I'll do better next time.

3. 새참, 분식, 간식 snacks/munchies

우리나라에는 참 다양한 먹을거리들이 있죠? 일하는 중간에 허기를 달래기 위해 먹는 새참, 떡볶이며 튀김 같은 분식과 간단하게 즐겨 먹는 간식까지! 이렇게 다양한 먹을거리를 가리키는 표현을 영어로 살펴보겠습니다. 가장 흔하게 snacks를 사용하고 가벼운 음식을 표현하기 위해 munchies라는 표현도 있습니다. 이밖에 마실 것들을 가리켜 refreshments라고 하고 간단하게 집어 먹을 수 있는 음식은 finger foods라고 하니까 같이 알아두세요.

A: Let's watch some TV and eat some munchies together.
B: Great idea. What kind of snacks do you have?

Exercises

• Grammar Practice

Follow the directions and complete the sentences.

1. Add a preposition.
    a. I'll put you _____ .
    b. I work _____ finance.
    c. What's Busan _____ ?
    d. Where are you _____ ?
    e. I'm so happy _____ you!
    f. It's difficult _____ tell the difference!

    | for | in | to | from | like | through |

2. Add a verb and complete each sentence.
    a. It's quite _____ .
    b. It sounds _____ .
    c. We're just _____ .
    d. Thanks for _____ .
    e. What are you _____ ?
    f. I _____ , I was eating snakes.

    | say | eat | crowd | look | come | confuse |

Tips for Studying

Stella [*To class.*]	So, tell me. **How do you practice English pronunciation?**
Soyeong	**I have been watching** English classes on OUN–TV and American TV shows with English subtitles.
Stella	**That's a good idea.** Have you ever seen American TV shows? That's a great way to study English.
Megan	I don't have enough time to watch TV because of my job. But I listen to MP3 downloads of English conversation while I'm on the bus or subway.
Stella	Ah, yes! That's the best way to use your time when you are commuting. What else? Let me know some other ways to improve your English.
Eric	I also try to learn by reading newspapers and magazines in English.
Stella	Those are also great study tools. **Just be sure to** memorize any new words you come across.
Ben	**It also helps to** make friends with English speakers.
Stella	Right. Using language in real life is the best way to improve your English. Remember: if you don't use it, you'll lose it!

Key Patterns

1. I have been _____ing _____.

   I have been watching English classes on OUN-TV.

2. If you _____. **If you** don't use it, you'll lose it.

3. How do you _____?

   How do you practice English pronunciation?

1

I have been _____ ing _____.

_____부터 계속 _____하고 있어요.

I have been watching English classes on OUN-TV.

복잡해 보이지만 꼭 알아두셔야 할 패턴으로 문법적인 용어로는 현재완료 진행이라고 합니다. Have 동사의 현재형 + be 동사 완료형 + 동사 진행형 ~ing를 사용합니다. Watch TV 'TV를 보다'를 예로 들면, 쭉 과거부터 현재까지 그리고 지금도 보고 있다는 뜻이 됩니다. 의외로 활용도가 높으니 꼭 기억하시도록!

I have been studying Japanese since I was 13.

저는 열세 살 이후로 지금까지 쭈욱 일본어를 공부해오고 있어요.

Daniel, my English teacher, has been living in Korea since 1998.

제 영어 선생님, 대니얼은 1998년 이후로 계속 한국에 거주하고 계세요.

2

If you _____.

만약 당신이 _____한다면.

If you don't use it, you'll lose it.

94

If 주어 + 동사, 즉 가정법입니다. 영어를 비롯해서 많은 경우, 사용하지 않으면 그냥 잃어버리는 능력들이 많죠?

If they run away, what should we do?

그들이 만약 도망쳤다면, 우리는 어떻게 하지?

If I were a carpenter, would you marry me?

제가 만일 목수라면, 저랑 결혼해주시겠어요?

그 외에도 다양한 표현이 가능합니다.

If this is true, I can't help you anymore.

이것이 사실이라면, 저는 이제 더 이상 당신을 도와드릴 수 없습니다.

What if I don't want to go out with you?

제가 당신과 데이트하고 싶지 않다면요?

I don't know if it's worth it.   그만큼 가치 있는 일인지 잘 모르겠어요.

3

How do you _____?   어떻게 _____를 한거야?

How do you practice English pronunciation?

How do you + 동사 구문을 넣어서, 상대편의 의견 혹은 방법을 묻는 표현입니다.

How do you know her, anyway?   그런데, 그녀를 어떻게 알고 있어?

How do you come up with these ideas?   어떻게 이런 생각을 해냈어?

A.   How do + 주어 + 동사~?는 "어떻게 ~할 수 있습니까?"라는 뜻입니다. 주어까지 바꾸어서 활용해보겠습니다.

How do we get to the subway station from here?

여기서 지하철역까지 어떻게 가요?

How do I win this game?   제가 어떻게 하면 이 경기에서 이길 수 있을까요?

Alternative Expressions

1 How do you practice your English skills?

= *What are ways to improve your English skills/pronunciation?*

= *How can you practice/improve your English skills?*

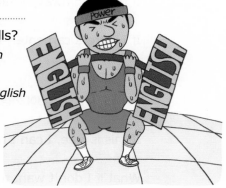

2 I have been watching~.

I like to watch~

I enjoy watching~

3 That's a good idea.

= *That's a good point.*

= *I see. That's very insightful.*

= *You make a good point.*

= *Exactly.*

= *Good point!*

= *That's true.*

= *Right.*

4 Just be sure to~

= *Make sure that you~*

= *Take care that you~*

= *Be careful that you~*

= *Please be sure to~*

5 It also helps to~

= *It's also helpful to~*

= *It's also good to~*

= *It's also advisable to~*

= *It's also wise to~*

Focus on Pronunciation

2. 과거형 −ed의 발음

유성음 다음에 −ed가 오면 /d/로 발음하고, 무성음 다음에 −ed가 오면 /t/로 발음합니다.

Cleaned, surprised, cared /d/

ex) I was so surprised at the news of Annie's pregnancy.

Asked, stepped, finished /t/

ex) They finished their assignment early.

주의할 것은 예외적으로, t나 d 다음에는 −ed를 /id/로 발음합니다.

Needed, landed, started /id/

ex) I needed you.
You needed me.

Real & Live

1. **비결이 뭐야?** What's your secret?

공부를 잘하는 사람들은 무언가 색다른 방법을 가지고 있는 것 같습니다. 이런 경우 비결이 무엇인지 물어보고 싶을 때 사용하시면 좋은 표현이 바로 secret입니다. 흔히 secret이라고 하면 비밀이라고 알고 있는데 자신만의 비밀이 비결이라고 할 수 있으니 우리말과 완전히 다른 것도 아니죠? 공부를 잘하는 친구, 요즘 들어 부쩍 예뻐지는 친구, 사업에서 성공 가도를 달리는 친구들에게 물어보세요! "What's your secret?"

> A: Shannon, your skin looks so smooth and clear.
>   What's your secret?
> B: Drink lots of water and use sunscreen.

2. **그는 공부벌레야.** He's a machine.

공부벌레라는 표현을 bookworm으로 알고 있는 분이 많을 거예요. 말 그대로 책을 많이 읽는 책벌레라는 표현이니까요. 그런데 우리가 공부벌레라고 할 때는 책을 많이 읽는 사람하고는 좀 다르죠. 공부벌레는 아침부터 밤늦게까지 변함없이 꾸준히 공부하는 사람을 뜻하죠. 그리고 우리는 좀 더 대학생활에 맞는 현대적인 표현으로 익혀보는 것도 중요하구요. 그래서 우리가 익혀야 할 표현은 바로

machine입니다. 기계라는 뜻이죠. 원래는 study machine이라고 하지만 machine만으로도, 기계처럼 꿈적도 하지 않고 공부만 하는 사람이란 뜻이 됩니다. 좀 실감나죠?

A: Charles has been studying for six hours straight!
And he's still there at the library.
B: He's a machine. That's why he does so well on his tests.

3. 제가 어디서 뵌 것 같은데요?

Excuse me, haven't I seen you somewhere before?

이 표현은 한국어에서도 유용하게 사용하는 표현이지요. 전혀 만나본 적이 없는 사람에게 다가가면서, '제가 어디선가 뵌 것 같은데요'라고 접근하는 거지요. 특히 문장에 앞서, excuse me라는 표현을 사용함으로써, 정중한 대화가 이어집니다. 물론, 언젠가 만난 적이 있는 사람과의 자연스러운 대화를 이끌어낼 때도 유용합니다.

A: Excuse me, haven't I seen you somewhere before?
B: Ah yes, we met last week at the opera. Jacob, right?
How are you?

Exercises

• Find the errors and make corrections

1. What do you eating?

2. I think, I am confuse.

3. How much these are?

4. It's a great place shopping.

5. Why are you look so sick?

6. If don't you use it, you will lose it.

7. That's a great way studying English.

8. Matthew and I go bar hopping last night.

9. I have been watch English class on OUN – TV.

10. I either have to cut down on my drinking and not drink at all.

Culture Corner

• Diversity

America has a long and complicated history of large−scale immigration involving peoples from many nations and cultures. As a result of this legacy, America has tremendous diversity in its population. Today, there are over 300 million people living in the U.S. who come from all over the world. America is truly a multi−ethnic and multicultural society. It has sometimes been called a "melting pot" of different races, ethnicities, and cultures. That is, the mass of immigrants learn to assimilate into mainstream society and "melt away" their differences. However, in recent decades, especially following the Civil Rights movement of the 1960s, some minority groups have challenged the notion of a melting pot and claim that immigrants should not necessarily have to give up certain traits of their culture, heritage or traditions.

There is a difference between the terms "race" and "ethnicity." The two terms are complicated and difficult to apply in a diverse society. Basically, race generally refers to broad, biological categories such as "White," "Asian," "African American," etc. On the other hand, "ethnicity" generally refers to a more specific category such as "Irish," "Polish," "Korean," "Nigerian" or "Vietnamese." Thus, for example, African Americans (at 12.8 percent) are the largest racial minority, but Hispanics and Latino Americans (who make up 15 percent of the population) are the largest ethnic minority in the U.S.

Today, White Americans currently remain the racial majority, but America is becoming an increasingly multiracial society. In 2009, President Barack Obama became the first African American president of the United States. His mother was from America and his father was from Kenya.

- **When did some minority groups begin to challenge the idea of a melting pot?**

- **Which race is the current majority in America?**

Theme V

Invitations

Lesson 10

Inviting Friends

Lesson 11

Surprise Party

Lesson 12

Potluck Dinner

In Theme V, presents scenes of invitation and celebration. Michael wishes to celebrate his birthday party. However, he is disappointed when both Soyeong and Alex say that they will be unable to attend. Discouraged, he invites Jennifer and her boyfriend Matthew, only to be surprised when Soyeong and Alex show up at his apartment with a cake. Michael and his friends enjoy a potluck dinner in celebration of his birthday.

Inviting Friends

Michael	Hey, **are you guys free this weekend?** I'm thinking of having a few friends over to my house for dinner.
Alex	I'm sorry, but I don't think I can make it. **I have plans** this weekend.
Soyeong	I'd love to, but I can't, either. I have final exams next week and I have to cram over the weekend. Sorry!
Michael	That's OK. I understand. Maybe next time, then.
Alex	Yes, definitely! Well, Soyeong and I have to do some gift shopping for a friend.
Michael	OK, see you around. [*Women leave; Michael calls Jennifer.*]
Jennifer	Michael! Hey, what's up?
Michael	Hey Jennifer. Listen, do you think you and Matthew can come over for dinner at my place this weekend?
Jennifer	Sure, we'd love to! But what's the matter? **You sound kind of down.**
Michael	Yeah, I guess I got a bit depressed just now. To be honest, it's my birthday and I wanted to celebrate with Soyeong and Alex, but **they just flaked out.** Nobody else can make it. Are you sure you're in?
Jennifer	I'm in. I wouldn't miss it for the world! Thanks for inviting me! Listen, is there anything I can bring?
Michael	**You don't have to bring anything but yourself!**

Key Patterns

1. I'm _____.   I'm in.

2. Nobody can _____.   Nobody else can make it.

3. What's up?   What's up?

1

I'm _____.

저는 _____ 하겠습니다.

I'm in.

I'm + 전치사입니다. 전치사로 그냥 끝나는 표현들을 먼저 살펴봅니다.

I'm in. 나는 할래.

He's out. 그는 졌어. 그는 나갔어. 그는 더 이상 하고 싶지 않대요.

You're out. 당신은 탈락입니다.

최근 많은 리얼리티 쇼에서 들어볼 수 있었던 표현입니다. "be in"은 '통과했다', '하고싶다' 는 표현으로 또한 "be out"은 '탈락했다', '기권했다' 는 뜻으로 사용됩니다. In과 out 전치사 다음에 명사를 넣을 수도 있습니다.

I'm in an English conversation club at university.

전 영어회화 클럽에 가입했어요.

I'm in trouble with my boyfriend.

남자친구랑 문제가 좀 있어요.

I'm not in the mood for dancing.

저는 춤추고 싶지 않아요.

2

Nobody can _____ . 다른 누구도 _____ 할 수 없어요.

Nobody else can make it.

Nobody는 no one 즉 none과 같은 뜻이죠. Nobody는 anybody/anyone, some body/someone과 함께 다양하게 활용할 수 있어야 합니다. 관용적으로 중요하지 않은 사람을 지칭하는 경우에 사용하기도 합니다.

I want nobody, nobody but you. 저는 꼭 당신을 원해요.

Don't worry about him. He's nobody.

그 사람에 대해서 걱정하지 마세요. 그 사람 뭐 그리 실세 아니에요.

Do you know her? She's someone. Watch out!

혹시 저 여성 알아요? 실세래요. 조심하세요!

3 What's up?

무슨 일이죠?

What's up?은 그냥 숙어처럼 통째로 외워두세요. 좀 친한 친구나 가까운 사이에서 안부를 묻거나, 오랜만에 만났을 때, 혹은 전화를 받으면서 Hello 대신에, 그리고 그냥 지나쳐가면서 인사할 수 있는 표현입니다.

What's up? What brought you here?

오랜만이야, 여긴 무슨 일로 왔어?

Hey, what's cooking?   와, 잘 지냈어?

How's it going?   잘 지내고 있어요?

What's new?   뭐 새로운 소식 있어요?

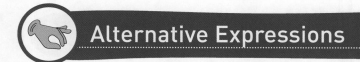

Alternative Expressions

1   Are you guys free this weekend?
= *What are you doing this weekend?*
= *Any plans this weekend?*

2   I have plans.
= *I have a prior engagement.*
= *I have a previous appointment.*

3   You sound kind of down.
= *You sound depressed.*
= *You sound beat.*
= *You sound out of it.*

4   They just flaked out.
= *They ditched me.*
= *They stood me up!*
= *They are flaky.*
= *They flaked.*

5   Host responses to "Should I bring anything [to a party]?"
If you'd like, you can bring something to drink.
That would be great. Please bring some wine.
OR:
Don't worry about it!

Focus on Pronunciation

• Part 5. 약 화

Flapping

American English(미국 영어)와 British English(영국 영어)의 자음 중에서 발음 차이가 느껴진다면, 특히 T/t/를 주목하세요. T 발음의 flapping 현상은 미국 영어의 가장 큰 특징입니다. 그러나 영국 영어는 T/t/가 자음 사이 혹은 모음 사이에 온다 하더라도, 발음상의 변화가 없습니다. 본 교재에서 교육용으로 선택한 언어가 미국 영어이므로, flapping 약화를 다룹니다. 소리 내어 연습하시기 바랍니다.

T가 모음 사이에 오는 경우, t 발음은 약화되어 /d/나 /r/처럼 발음합니다. (단, 강세가 앞에 있는 경우)

later, city, water, butter, writer
attend – 강세가 뒤에 있으므로 flapping이 되지 않습니다.

본문 속 예문

What's the matter?
Thanks for inviting me!

Real & Live

1. 나 바람맞았어. I'm being stood up.

누군가와 데이트 약속을 했는데 그 혹은 그
녀가 약속 장소에 나타나지 않은 경우, 흔히
'바람을 맞았다' 라는 표현을 사용하죠. 누군
가가 어느 장소에 나를 그대로 세워놓았다는
표현인데, 결국 안 나타났으니까 '바람을 맞
았다' 라는 뜻이 되는 겁니다.

She stood me up.

(그녀가 나를 바람맞혔어.)

She's making me wait for her.

(그녀는 내가 그녀를 기다리게 해놓고는 나타나지 않았어.)

A: Hey Helen, how did your date go last night?
B: Terrible! He stood me up.
   I finally left and went home after waiting for an hour.

2. 네가 나한테 어떻게 그럴 수 있니? How can you do that to me?

상대편에게 억울한 심정이 들 때 사용하는 표현입니다. 여기서는 this나 that을 사용하는 것에 큰 차이는 없고, 억양을 살려서 '정말 어떻게 이럴 수 있어!' 라는 느낌을 살려서 사용해보도록 하세요.

> How can you do that to me? (네가 나한테 어떻게 이럴 수 있니?)
> How could you do this to me? (제게 어떻게 이러실 수 있어요?)

A: Honey, I'm so sorry I forgot to wake you up before I left to take a walk.
B: How could you do this to me? You knew I wanted to go walking together with you!

3. 제 입장에서 생각해주세요. Please put yourself in my shoes.

억울한 일이 있을 때 흔히들 '내 입장 좀 생각해줘' 라고 말하죠. 영어로는 '당신이 직접 내 신발을 신어보세요' 라고 합니다. 입장 혹은 처지를 영어에선 신발로 표현하는 것이 흥미롭지 않습니까? 이 표현이 나의 처지를 고려해달라고 하는 표현이라면 상대편의 입장을 고려해달라고 할 때는 "Just to play devil's advocate"라고 합니다. 악마를 변호한다고 하니 이 표현 또한 재미난 표현이라고 생각되는데요, 어떤 입장에서든지 억울함을 호소하고 싶을 때 이 표현들을 적절히 사용하시면 정말 유용할 것 같습니다.

A: I really don't understand him. He's such a jerk.
B: Please try to put yourself in his shoes.
   He has been under a lot of stress these days.

Exercises

Match Up Words and Meaning

Words	Meaning
1. free	A. Feel sad
2. gift	B. Truthful or sincere
3. miss	C. Talk about it in detail
4. invite	D. To ask someone to attend
5. honest	E. To fail to hit, reach, or contact
6. discuss	F. Not restricted, controlled, or limited
7. confuse	G. Complicated or difficult to understand
8. definitely	H. The way in which things are unlike each other
9. depressed	I. Something that you give to someone as a present
10. difference	J. A way that emphasizes the strength of your intention or opinion

Surprise Party

Jennifer and Matthew   Hey! Happy Birthday!

Michael   Hey, guys! **Come on in.** Thanks for coming.

Jennifer   Here, we brought you something. It's just a little something. I hope you like it.

Michael   Aw, you really shouldn't have. Ah, a travel guidebook! This is exactly what I've been looking for! Thanks!

● Doorbell rings; Michael opens door; Soyeong and Alex appear smiling.

Michael   Soyeong? Alex? What brings you guys here?

Soyeong and Alex   Surprise!

Michael   What's going on?

Soyeong   We knew it was your birthday! We just wanted to surprise you! Here's a present for you!

Alex   Here! This is for you, too!

Michael   **I can't believe this!** Thanks, guys! Come on in, come on in! Have a seat, **make yourselves comfortable!**

Soyeong   **I hope we didn't scare you!** Come on, let's celebrate!

Michael   I'm so glad you guys could make it. Really. **Let me get you something to drink!**

Key Patterns

1. I hope (that) _____. I **hope** you like it.
2. Let me _____.
   Let me get you something to drink!
3. What brings _____? **What brings** you guys here?

1

I hope (that) _____. 저는 _____를 기원합니다.
I hope you like it.

Hope는 말 그대로 바라다, 희망하다, 기원하다 등의 뜻입니다. 뒤에 that 절이 오는 경우가 일반적이며, 간혹 I hope to see you soon에서처럼 to 부정사를 사용하는 굳어진 표현들도 사용됩니다.

I hope (that) you're getting better soon.
당신의 건강이 좋아지시길 바랄게요. 쾌유하시길 빌어요.
I hope you can make it to the Ph.D. program.
박사 과정에 입학하시길 기원하겠습니다.

Let me _____.

제가 한번 _____ 해볼게요.

Let me get you something to drink!

Let me + 동사는 "내가 한번 해볼게"라는 뜻의 가벼운 제안입니다. I'll + 동사처럼 의지를 불태우는 경우도 아니고, let을 사용해서 상대편을 배려하고 있는 느낌도 나니, 활용해볼 만하죠?

Let me get you home.

집에 바래다드릴게요.

Let me see your driver's license, please.

운전면허증 좀 보여주시겠어요?

Let me tell you something interesting.

재미있는 얘기 해줄까?

What brings _____? 무슨 일로 _____ 했어요?

What brings you guys here?

"여기는 무슨 일로 왔어요?"의 가장 자연스러운 표현으로 "What brings you guys here?"을 소개합니다. 장소나 상황을 한국어로 먼저 생각하면서, here…you…come…where…. 뭐 이렇게 복잡하게 영작하지 마세요.

What brings you here?

무슨 일이야?

Hello, what brought you here in the middle of the night?

아이고, 이렇게 늦은 밤에 무슨 일로 여기까지 왔어요?

A. What makes + you _____?를 확대해볼까요?

What makes you happy now?

무슨 좋은 일 있어?

She doesn't look good.

그녀의 표정이 안 좋은걸.

What makes her so sad?

그녀는 무슨 일로 저렇게 슬퍼?

Alternative Expressions

1   Come on in.
  - = *So nice of you to come!*
  - = *Welcome! Please come [on] in!*

2   I can't believe this!
  - = *I feel like I'm dreaming!*
  - = *What a surprise!*
  - = *This is awesome!*
  - = *This is great!*

3   Make yourselves comfortable!
  - = *Make yourselves at home!*
  - = *Please help yourself.*
  - = *Help yourself.*

4   I hope we didn't scare you!
  - = *I hope we didn't startle you.*
  - = *I hope we didn't embarrass you too much!*
  - = *Sorry to embarrass you!*

5   Let me get you something to drink!
  - = *Would you like something to drink?*
  - = *Can I get you something to drink?*
  - = *I/We have snacks in the fridge/in the kitchen.*

H의 약화

이 발음도 미국 영어에서 특히 많이 나타나는 현상입니다. 문장의 중간에 오는 인칭대명사, 조동사, 부사 등의 h는 발음이 약화되어 힘없이 발음하거나 발음하지 않습니다. 기본적으로 기능어를 워낙 약하게 발음하다보니, 잘 안 들리게 됩니다.

인칭 대명사: He, him, her, his…
조동사: Have, has…
부사: Here…

Please tell him.
Bring her over here.

본문 속 예문

What brings you guys here?

예문뿐만 아니라, 다른 예로 등장한 him, her 등의 h를 거의 발음하지 않고, 큰 소리로 읽어봅시다.

1. 어쩐지 오늘 네가 올 것 같은 예감이 들었어.

I had a hunch that you would come today.

'어쩐지 ~한 예감' 이라는 표현을 할 때에 보통 feeling이라는 단어를 가장 많이 사용합니다. Real & Live에서는 좀 더 생생한 느낌을 살릴 수 있는 hunch라는 단어를 사용한 문장을 소개해드립니다. Hunch는 예감, 육감을 뜻하는 단어로 꼽추의 등에 닿으면 행운이 온다는 미신에서 비롯된 단어라고 합니다. 이제부터는 어쩐지 뭔가 독특한 그런 예감이 들었다고 말하고 싶다면 hunch를 이용해보세요. 여러분의 표현을 좀 더 생동감 있게 전할 수 있을 겁니다.

A: Hi, it's me! Are you surprised to see me?
B: Actually, I had a hunch you would come today.

2. 기분 정말 끝내줘! I'm flying high.

정말 기분이 좋아 날아갈 것 같다는 말이 되겠죠? 나 저 위로 높이 날아가고 있어! 우리말에서도 똑같은 표현을 쓰는데요, 이 밖에도 기분이 좋을 때 쓰는 여러 가지 표현들을 살펴볼까요?

I'm as happy as a clam.

매우 기쁘고 만족한다는 표현입니다. 조개의 입 모양과 행복해서 크게 미소 짓고 있는 사람의 입모양이 비슷하다고 하여 나온 표현입니다. 절대 조개만큼 행복하다고 해석하지 마세요!

I'm feeling like a million bucks.

Buck은 달러(dollar)를 뜻하는 말입니다. 백만 달러의 가치가 있는 사람으로 느껴진다는 표현인데요, 보통 영어 표현에서 백만 달러는 매우 큰 돈을 의미하기 때문에 자신의 감정을 그만큼 큰 값어치에 비유한다는 것은 자기 자신이나 처한 상황이 그만큼 만족스럽다는 것을 의미합니다.

A: John, what's up? You look so happy!
B: I'm flying high! I just got an A on my midterm exam!

3. 너밖에 없어! You're the best!

정말 소중한 친구에게 '너 없으면 안 된다'는 의미로 네가 최고라고 영어로는 표현합니다. 우리말에서의 너밖에 없다는 의미보다 조금 약한 감은 있지만 the best보다 더 좋은 것은 없겠죠?

A: Sarah, I thought about it and decided to let you have my car for free. Here are the keys.
B: Really? Jane, you're the best! Thank you!

Exercises

Crossword Puzzle

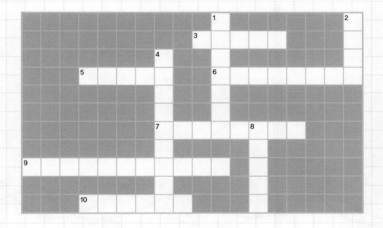

Down

1. Something that you give to someone, for example at Christmas or when you visit
2. A feeling of desire and expectation that things will go well in the future
4. To do something enjoyable because of a special occasion or to mark someone's success
8. When you _____ water, you take it into your mouth and swallow it

Across

3. To take someone or something with you
5. If something _____ you, it frightens you
6. The feeling that you have when something unexpected happens
7. The date on which you were born
9. To feel physically or emotionally satisfied or relaxed
10. If you _____, you go from one place to another, often to a place that is far away

Potluck Dinner

Jennifer   Hey, Michael. Where can I put this? I brought some wine and cheese.

Michael   Wonderful! There's a table in the dining room. **You can set them over there.**

Alex   I'm starving! I need something to fill me up.

Soyeong   **You should eat some of these.** See? I brought some *kim bop*.

Michael   Hey, everybody. I also prepared some salad and pasta in the kitchen. Help yourself!

Jennifer   Oh! Pasta? That sounds yummy.

● Everybody goes to the kitchen.

Soyeong   This pasta smells so good. [*Takes a bite of salad.*] And these tomatoes **taste so fresh!**

Jennifer   Mmmm, this is the best pasta I've had in a long time. You're a good cook, Michael!

Alex   Hey, let's open that bottle of wine! And **can somebody hand me another plate of spaghetti,** please?

Michael   Are you sure you want to drink so soon after your hangover last week?

Alex   This is a party! And anyway, a glass of wine a day is good for your health.

Key Patterns

1. I'm ＿＿＿＿＿＿＿＿ ing.   I'm starving!

2. It is good for ＿＿＿＿＿＿＿.
   A glass of wine a day **is good for** your health.

3. Where can I ＿＿＿＿＿＿＿?   **Where can I** put this?

1

I'm ＿＿＿＿＿＿＿＿＿＿ing.

저는 ＿＿＿＿＿＿＿＿ 하고 있어요.

I'm starving!

늘 배가 고프다는 표현을 "I'm hungry"라고 사용하셨죠? 배가 고파서 죽을 것처럼 조금 과장해서 "나 굶어 죽을 것 같아"라고 했습니다. I'm + 형용사뿐만 아니라 I'm + 동사 ing 표현을 연습해보세요.

I'm thirsty.

목 말라.

I'm craving for something.

뭐든 먹을 수 있을 것 같아.

2

It is good for _____. _____ 하는 것은 효과적입니다.
A glass of wine a day is good for your health.

다양한 뜻으로 사용되는 good이 이번에는 for와 함께 "효율적인, 효과적인"의 뜻으로 사용되었습니다. "It's good for you"라고 하면 "당신에게 도움이 될 거예요"라는 뜻이 되죠. 그 외에도 다양한 뜻을 살펴봅시다.

The *bibimbap* is good here. 이 집은 비빔밥을 잘해요.
Is 2:00 p.m. good for you? 2시면 괜찮으세요?
The Internet is good for learners of English as a foreign language.
인터넷은 영어를 외국어로 배우는 학습자들에게 유용하다.

3

Where can I _____? 제가 어디에 _____ 할까요?
Where can I put this?

Where 조동사 + 주어 + 동사?로 장소에 대한 의문문을 연습해봅니다.

Where are you going now? 당신 지금 어딜 가시는 거예요?
Where should we stay? 우리는 어디에 머물러야 합니까?

Alternative Expressions

1 You can set them over there.
= *Anywhere is fine.*
= *Please put them over there.*
= *Please set them on the table.*
= *You can place them over there.*

2 You should eat some of these.
= *Please try some.*
= *Have a bite [of these]!*
= *Take a bite!*
= *Grab a handful* [cookies, chips, popcorn, etc.]

3 Tastes so fresh!
Tasty!
Mmmmm!
These taste:
salty
sweet
sour
spicy
hot
buttery
nutty
juicy
savory: not sweet, but piquant and full — flavored

4   Can somebody hand me another plate of spaghetti?

May I have a napkin/fork/spoon/plate, please?

Could you hand me a napkin?

Pass the salt/pepper, please.

Could I get another refill?

5   "seconds": a second helping (see also, "thirds"=third serving of food)

These are so good! I'm going for seconds!

Liquids/drinks:	*carton*	*can*	*pitcher*	*bottle*	
Food:	*jar*	*plate*	*dish of~*	*container of~*	*bag of~*

A carton of milk

A jar of pickles

A bag of potato chips

A container of potato salad

And의 발음

대표적인 접속사인 and는 문장의 가장 앞에 오는 경우에는 /ænd/로 모두 발음되지만, 문장의 중간에 오는 경우는 약화되어 /and/ 대신에 /n/ 정도로 발음되는 경우가 많습니다.

You and me
Salt and pepper
Rock and roll

본문 속 예문

And these tomatoes taste so fresh!
I brought some kim bop and japchae.
I also prepared some salad and pasta in the kitchen.

130

1. 너무 배부르다. I'm stuffed.

'stuffed'는 '속이 무언가로 꽉차다' 라는 뜻입니다. 맛있는 것을 많이 먹어서, 배가 부를 때 다른 표현으로 "I'm so full." 이렇게도 이야기할 수 있겠지요. 재미있는 것은 stuffed animals라는 표현인데요, 속이 꽉 찬 동물은 또 뭘까요? Teddy bear 곰 인형이나 털 인형처럼 속이 푹신푹신한 인형들을 영어로 stuffed animal이라고 한답니다.

A: Would you like some more?
B: No thank you, I'm stuffed!

2. 1/n로 나눠 계산하자. Everybody chips in.

여럿이 모여 맛있는 음식을 먹을 때 누군가 "내가 쏠께!" 하면 좋겠지만 대부분의 경우에는 전체 금액을 사람 수만큼 나눠서 계산을 하죠. Chip은 자르다, 쪼개다의 의미가 있는데 총 액수를 사람 수로 자른다, 쪼갠다라고 생각을 하면 어렵지 않으실 거예요. 단, 이 표현은 우리가 생각하는 더치페이와는 약간 차이가 있습니다. 더치페이는 말 그대로 자신이 먹은 음식값만 계산하는 거죠. 그렇다면 더치페이, 즉 각자 내자는 말은 어떻게 하는지 바로 살펴볼까요?

A: I'm going to buy a birthday gift for Alex and I am asking everybody to chip in.
B: I'll chip in five dollars. Here you go.

3. 각자 내죠. Let's split the check.

많은 분들이 각자 비용을 지불하자는 표현으로 "더치페이하자"라고 합니다. 영어로 Dutch pay가 되는데, 물론 역사적으로는 상업과 무역을 중시했던 네덜란드 사람들이 물건이나 식사 등의 비용을 각자 지불하는 것에서 왔다고 설명하지요. 그런데 막상 Dutch pay라는 영어 표현은 거의 사용하지 않습니다. 굳이 Dutch를 사용하고 싶으면, 오히려 "Let's go Dutch"라고 하지요.

그리고 Real & Live에서는 "각자 내죠"를 더 생생한 표현으로 알려드립니다. Split이라는 표현이 '반으로 자르다/가르다'는 것은 잘 아시죠?

Let's get separate checks. /Let's split the check.

결국, Let's split the check! 하게 되면, "영수증을 각자로 나누어주세요"라는 뜻이 되니까, 바로 우리가 하고 싶었던 말, "각자 냅시다"가 됩니다. 우리 한국 문화는 연장자가 많은 경우 비용을 지불했어요. 그러나 요즘, 젊고 어린 연령층으로 갈수록 "각자 먹은 만큼/혹은 마신 만큼 냅시다"라는 표현을 쉽게 접할 수 있습니다.

A: Let's see... The bill for the meal comes out to be $24.
B: Let's split this. Here's $12.

Exercises

• Choosing the Word

Fill in the blanks with the best possible expressions from the list. Pay attention to how the expressions are used grammatically. You may need to consider verb tenses, subject–verb agreement, etc.

something to eat	go for anything
Let's see	would be fine
how to use	prefer
feel like	free time
also	would

Jacob: Do you have (1)_____? I'm hungry.

Emily: Yeah, let's get (2)_____.

Jacob: (3)_____... Where should we go?

Emily: Hmmm... What (4)_____you like?

Jacob: Oh, I could (5)_____.

Emily: Well, I like spicy food, so I (6)_____eating Korean food.

Jacob: That (7)_____.

Emily: Have you ever had *samgyeopsal* before?

Jacob: Yes, I love it. But I (8)_____Korean barbecue.

Emily: Do you know (9)_____chopsticks?

Jacob: Yes! I (10)_____know how to eat spicy foods!

Here are just a few of the major holidays celebrated in the United States:

* **January 1**
New Year's Day. People usually celebrate at New Year's parties by counting down the final seconds to midnight (12:00 AM) on New Year's Eve (December 31). People usually make New Year's Resolutions which are promises to change or improve one's life.

* **February 14**
Valentines Day. The traditional day of romance between couples. This day usually involves the exchange of gifts, flowers, and candy.

* **Sunday in Late March/Late April (varies)**
Easter. This day celebrates the resurrection of Jesus. Many Christian families gather together at churches to attend service. Children will decorate and color eggs, go on Easter egg hunts and eat chocolate eggs and chocoloate bunnies. Like Santa Claus, the Easter Bunny traditionally comes to give colored eggs and toys to children.

* **Fourth Thursday in November**
Thanksgiving. In America, families get together for a turkey dinner in a tradition that started when the first English settlers arrived to the American colonies in the 1600s. The American tradition is often

thought to have started in 1621 when the English Pilgrims in Plymouth, Massachusetts received help with food and farming from Native Americans after a very hard winter. In Canada, Thanksgiving is celebrated on the second Monday in October.

* **December 25**

Christmas Day. Originally celebrated to mark the birth of Jesus, Christmas has become a largely secular holiday celebrated by non – Christians throughout the entire nation. Christmas Day is often spent with family and with exchanging gifts and cards. Traditionally, Santa Claus comes to visit the homes of children on Christmas Eve (December 24) and leaves presents for them under the Christmas tree.

Theme VI

Travel

In Theme VI, we see that Michael is planning a vacation in South Korea. After hearing recommendations from Alex and Soyeong, he attempts to reserve a hotel room, but has some difficulty. In the final lesson, Alex is departing for a few weeks in the United States and says goodbye to Soyeong, who is now his girlfriend.

Planning Vacations

Michael	So Alex, **any vacation plans?**
Alex	I was planning to visit San Francisco for a few weeks. **Interested in joining me there?**
Michael	I was planning to stay here in Korea during my break. But I can't decide where to go. **Do you have any recommendations?**
Soyeong	Hmmm⋯. Have you been to Busan?
Michael	No. **What is there to see over there?**
Alex	In my opinion, I'd say that you should definitely check out Haeundae Beach.
Soyeong	That's true. No trip to Busan would be complete without going there. The seafood down there is also very fresh and delicious. When do you plan on going?
Michael	I was thinking sometime this month.
Alex	And how long do you plan to be on vacation?
Michael	About a week or so.
Alex	Then you should make arrangements in advance. The tourist season can be quite hectic.
Soyeong	Yes, **it's better to make reservations now** than to try and book a hotel once you're there. I'll help you!

Key Patterns

1. I was _____ ing.
   I was planning to visit San Francisco for a few weeks.

2. **It's better (to) A than B.**
   It's better to make reservations now than to try and book
   a hotel once you're there.

3. **How long do you** _____?

   How long do you plan to be on vacation?

1

I was _____ing. 저는 _____ 하는 중이었어요.
I was planning to visit San Francisco for a few weeks.

I + be동사 과거형+ 동사~ing 진행형으로 과거진행
형 문장입니다. 영어는 의외로 동사의 일반형보
다는 진행형이나 분사형을 많이 사용합니다.
그리고 현재/과거진행형 문장과 현재/과거
완료 문장들이 더욱더 생동감 있는 표현
을 만들어낸다는 점 기억하세요.

I was wondering whether
you can make it to tonight's
premiere.

저는 당신이 오늘밤 시사회에 오실 수 있을지
궁금했습니다.

It's better to A than B.

B보다는 A하는 것이 더 좋습니다.

It's better to make reservations now than to try and book a hotel once you're there.

It's better A + than B 문장입니다. A하는 것이 B보다는 낫다는 거죠. 특히 이번 패턴에서는 단순한 명사 대신 to 부정사 구문을 A와 B 사이에 넣는 연습을 해보십시오.

It's better to give than to receive.

받는 것보다는 주는 것이 나아요.

It's better to do and regret than not to do at all.

아예 시도하지 않은 것보다는 하고 후회하는 것이 낫다.

How long do you _____?

_____ 하는 데 얼마나 걸리세요?

How long do you plan to be on vacation?

본문에 나온 문장은 How long do you + 동사_____?로 "당신이 _____ 하는 데 얼마나 기간을 잡으시나요?"라는 문장입니다. 주어를 I로도 바꿔서 문장을 만들어봅니다.

How long do you practice martial arts a day?

무술 연습은 얼마나 하세요?

How long do I have to wait?

제가 얼마나 기다려야 하죠?

How long does it take to + 동사? 유형은 "_____ 하는 데 얼마나 걸리죠?"
라는 주로 기간에 대한 의문문으로 자주 사용할 수 있는 표현입니다.

How long does it take to go to Gwanghwamun?
광화문까지 얼마나 걸려요?
How long does it take to knit a muffler?
머플러 하나 뜨는 데 얼마나 걸려요?
How long does it take to finish the job?
그 작업 끝내려면 얼마나 걸리실 것 같으신가요?

Alternative Expressions

---

1   Any vacation plans?
= *Where do you plan on going for vacation?*
= *Where are you going to go for your vacation?*
= *Planning on traveling/going anywhere?*
= *Are you planning on traveling anywhere this summer?*
= *Do you plan on going anywhere for your break?*
= *Any plans for the holiday/weekend/your vacation?*
= *Any travel plans?*

---

2   Interested in joining me there?
= *Would you like/care to join me?*
= *Would you like to go together?*
= *Why don't we go together?*

---

3   Do you have any recommendations?
= *Any places you would recommend?*
= *Any ideas/suggestions?*
= *Any advice on where to go?*
= *Which places would you recommend?*
= *Any vacation spots worth going to?*
= *Any suggestions?*

---

4   What is there to see over there?
= *What's so special about Gyeongsang Province?*
= *What is there to do over there?*
= *Is there anything worth seeing/checking out?*

---

5   It's better to make reservations now.
= *You should make advanced reservations.*
= *You should make reservations in advance.*
= *You should book your tickets early.*
= *You should try to get your tickets early.*

Focus on Pronunciation

Stress in Noun/Verb pairs (명전 동후)

같은 단어가 명사의 의미와 동사의 의미를 함께 갖는 경우, 명사로 쓰일 때는 강세를 앞(前)에, 동사로 쓰일 때는 강세를 뒤(後)에 발음합니다.

Noun vs. Verbs

❶ present (a gift)   present (to give ; to show)
❷ record (a recording)   record (to write down)
❸ convict (a criminal)   convict (to find guilty)

문장으로 연습해볼까요?

The organizing committee will present the prizes to the winners.
Please keep a record of all your payments.

Real & Live

1. 바람이나 쐬러 가자! Let's take a road trip!

이번 Real & Live에서는 "road"를 사용해서 여행과 관련 있는 표현들을 살펴보도록 하겠습니다. 첫 번째 표현은 "Let's take a road trip!"입니다. 영어에서 road trip이라고 하면 자동차를 타고 계획 없이 즉흥적으로 어딘가로 떠나는 것을 의미합니다. 그러므로 우리가 흔히 '바람이나 쐬자', '드라이브나 가자'라고 하는 것은 영어로 "Let's take a road trip!"이라고 할 수 있는 거죠.

> A: I'm bored. Let's take a road trip!
> B: Great idea. I'll get a map and get the car ready.

2. 출발하자고! Let's hit the road!

대개 '출발!', '가자!'라고 말을 할 때 "Let's go!"라고 하죠? 이제부턴 이렇게 말해보세요. 'hit the road'는 말 그대로 '땅을 박차고 나가다'라는 뜻입니다. 그래서 구어적인 표현으로 '가자', '떠나자' 등의 뜻이 됩니다. 또한 '시작하자'라는 뜻도 가집니다. 여기서 hit은 '~를 시작할 것을 의도하다'는 뜻으로 쓰였습니다. 따라서 상황에 따라 여러 의미로 사용되며 유용하게 쓰일 수 있는 좋은 표현입니다.

A: Well guys, this is the last rest stop on the highway for the next
   90 miles. Did everybody get a chance to use the restroom?
B: Yeah, we're all finished. Let's hit the road!

3. 여행 중이야! I'm on the road.

마지막 "road"를 사용한 여행 관련 표현은 "I'm on the road"입니다. 'on'이라는 전치사는 '~위에'라는 의미를 가지고 있어 '난 길 위에 있어' 즉, 여행 중이라는 표현이 되는 겁니다. 이렇게 "road"라는 단어 하나만 가지고도 여러 가지 다양한 표현들을 만들수 있다는 게 정말 재밌지 않나요?

A: Hello, Steve? Sorry to call you on your cell phone.
   Do you have a minute to talk?
B: Sorry Bill, but I'm on the road right now.
   Let me call you back when we pull over at the next rest stop.

Exercises

● Grammar Practice

Follow the directions and complete the sentences.

1. Add a preposition.
   a. This is _____ you!
   b. How long do you plan to be _____ vacation?
   c. I wanted to celebrate _____ Soyeong and Alex.
   d. This is the best pasta I've had _____ a long time!
   e. A glass of wine a day is good _____ your health.
   f. I have been watching English class _____ OUN‒TV.

   | in | on | for | for | on | with |

2. Add a verb and complete each sentence(You may have to change the tense or form).
   a. What's _____ on?
   b. We _____ it was your birthday!
   c. I was _____ to visit San Francisco.
   d. Have you ever _____ American TV shows?
   e. I'm _____ of having friends over to my house.
   f. _____ language is the best way to improve English.

   | see | think | go | plan | use | knew |

Making Reservations

Hotel Clerk A	Hello, Haeundae Hotel reservation desk, Vicky speaking. How may I help you?
Michael	Yes, **is it possible** to make a reservation on the 17th?
Clerk A	Certainly, sir. **And how many people will be traveling with you?** We have single rooms, double rooms, and suites.
Michael	Just myself.
Clerk A	And how long do you plan on staying with us, sir?
Michael	I am thinking of staying until the 21st.
Clerk A	I'm so sorry, sir. But I am afraid that **we are completely booked** after the 20th. **May I suggest you try another hotel?**

* * * *

Hotel Clerk B	This is the Busan Hotel, how may I help you?
Michael	Hi. Do you have a single room from the 17th to the 21st of this month? And I would prefer to stay in a room with **an ocean view.**
Clerk B	One moment, sir and I will check for you. Yes, we have a room available on those dates. Shall I reserve that for you, sir?
Michael	Yes, please!
Clerk B	So that will be one room with an ocean view for four full nights beginning on the 17th to the 21st of this month. And what time would you like to check in on the 17th? In the morning, afternoon or evening?
Michael	I would prefer to check in during the afternoon.

Key Patterns

1. I would prefer to _____.
   I would prefer to stay in a room with an ocean view.

2. That'll be _____.
   That will be one room for four full nights.

3. What time would you like to _____?
   What time would you like to check in?

1

I would prefer to _____.

저는 _____ 하는 편이 더 좋겠습니다.

I would prefer to stay in a room with an ocean view.

이 문형에서는 I would 즉 '공손
하게 하고 싶다'는 뜻의 조동사와
prefer to '~하는 것이 더 좋겠
다'는 동사까지 두 가지를 같이
익혀봅니다.

I would _____.

저는 _____ 하겠습니다.

**I would like to work with
you if possible.**

가능하면 나는 당신과 일하겠어요.

I wouldn't hurt you.

저는 당신을 힘들게 하지 않겠어요.

I prefer to _____.

차라리 _____ 편이 더 좋습니다.

I prefer to go now.

차라리 지금 갈래요.

I would prefer to have a meeting this week rather than next week.

다음주보다는 이번주에 회의를 하는 것이 더 좋습니다.

2

That'll be _____.

그럼 _____ 가 되겠습니다.

That will be one room for four full nights.

That will be + 명사는 "~ 되겠습니다"라는 표현으로 가격이나 흥정 등은 물론, 마무리를 정리하는 표현이 되겠지요.

That'll be $279.00 total.   합계 279달러가 되겠습니다.
Then, that'll be a standard (room) for one night.

네, 일반실 1박입니다.

3

What time would you like to _____?

몇 시에 _____ 하시겠습니까?

What time would you like to check in?

A.   What time would you like to _____? 공손하게 "몇 시쯤 _____ 하시겠어요?" 묻는 의문문으로 동사를 바꾸면 다양한 표현이 가능합니다.

What time would you like to go to the concert?   음악회 언제 갈까요?
What time would you like to make a speech?   연설은 몇 시쯤 하시겠습니까?

B. What time + 동사 + 주어~?는 시간 약속 등을 위해서 유용하게 사용되겠죠?

What time is it?

지금 몇 시예요?

What time are we going to meet this afternoon?

오후 몇 시에 만날까?

C. What + 명사 + 동사 + 주어~?로 확대하면 무궁무진한 표현이 가능해집니다.

What grade are you in?

몇 학년이에요?

What program are you interested in?

어떤 과정에 관심을 갖고 계십니까?

Alternative Expressions

1

Is it possible~?
= *Can I~?*
= *I'd like to~?*

2

How many people will be traveling with you?
How many in your party?
Will you be traveling alone?

3

We are completely booked.
= *We're completely sold out.*
= *All seats/rooms have been booked/*
  reserved/sold.
= *We're completely full.*
= *There are no rooms available.*
  [Signs and notices:]
= No Vacancy
= Sold Out

4

May I suggest you try another hotel?
= *Would you like to try another hotel?*
= *May I suggest another hotel?*

5

aisle seats
bulkhead seats [airplane]
seat near the exit
seat near the rear/to the rear of the theater
window seat
ocean –side view

접미사와 접두사가 있는 단어의 강세

접미사가 붙는 경우 대부분 강세가 이동하여 접미사 바로 앞 음절에 붙습니다.

Drama – Dramatic
Comedy – Comedian
Educate – Education

일반적으로 접두사에는 강세가 붙지 않습니다.

predict, precaution, review

하지만 동사와 명세를 함께 가지는 단어는, 명전동후의 규칙에 따라 발음합니다.

project : 명사일 경우 Project
Let's finish this project.

동사일 경우 Project

본문 속 예문

Is it possible to make a reservation on the 17th?
Shall I reserve that for you sir?

1. **아침 식사 포함되나요?** Does that include breakfast?

여행을 갈 때 숙소 예약은 필수죠. 숙
소 예약 시 가격에 대해 말할 때, 그
숙박료에 숙박뿐만 아니라 다음날 아
침 식사 비용까지 포함되어 있는지를
물어보는 표현입니다. 대개는 다음날
아침 식사 비용이 포함되어 있으나
간혹 없는 경우도 있으니 꼭 한 번
물어봐야 할 표현이겠죠? 보통 이렇
게 숙박 다음날 아침식사를 주는 숙
박업체들 앞에는 'Breakfast
Included'라고 쓰인 간판이나 현수
막과 같은 것을 볼 수 있습니다.

A: Here are the keys to your room, sir.
   The orientation will begin at 9 a.m. in the lobby.
B: Does that include breakfast?

2. **B&B에 가서 주말을 보낼 계획이야.**
   I'm planning to spend the weekend at a bed and breakfast.

앞서 설명한 것처럼 아침 식사가 포함된 숙박 서비스를 제공하는 호텔 등의 숙박업체들을
가리켜 'bed and breakfast'라고 합니다. 그리고 보통은 이를 줄여서 짧게 'B&B'라고

부릅니다. 외국에서는 개인 가정에서도 이런 서비스를 제공해주는 경우가 있습니다.

A: Any plans for this weekend?
B: Yes, my husband and I are going on a road trip to the countryside.
   We're planning to spend the weekend at a bed and breakfast.

3. 직원이 무척 친절해요. The clerk is so good to me.

Good, 즉 좋다는 단어를 좀 더 세련된, '배려하다, 잘해주다' 라는 뜻으로 사용하는 경우를 알아볼까요? 상대편이 여러분에게 잘해준다는 것은, 결국 배려에서 오는 거예요. 그런 '배려하다'는 표현이 'be good to someone' 이구요. "Be good to each other" 또는 "서로 배려하시고, 잘해주세요"라는 뜻으로 사용해봅시다.

Be good to yourself. 당신 스스로를 돌보세요.
I'm good to myself. 저는 저 자신을 소중하게 생각합니다.

자신을 소중하게 돌보고 사랑하는 사람이야말로, 다른 사람을 잘 돌보고, 사랑할 수 있다고 합니다. "Be good to yourself because nobody else has the power to make you happy." George Michael이라는 영국 가수가 부르는 "Heal the pain"이라는 노래에 나오는 가사입니다. 정말 멋지죠?

A: How was that new restaurant you tried yesterday?
B: The service was great! The waiter was so good to me.
   He gave us free appetizers and free refills!

Exercises

• Reorder the Sentences

Place the following sentences in the proper chronological order.

① Just one. Myself.

② Oh, good. I'll take the 9:15 train.

③ Certainly, sir. How many passengers?

④ And what date would you like to depart?

⑤ Is it possible to reserve a ticket to Mokpo?

⑥ I am thinking of leaving on July 13th in the morning.

⑦ Hello, thank you for calling Korean Railroad.
   How may I help you?

⑧ Please hold while I check the schedule.
   (pause) Sir, we have trains leaving at 8:45 and at 9:15 from Seoul Station.

Lesson 15

Saying Good-bye

Alex **Look at that view!**

Soyeong Isn't it thrilling? Look over there. There's Myeongdong!

Alex Ah, right. There it is. And where is the famous 63 Building?

Soyeong It's over there. That used to be the tallest building in Korea.

Alex It's really quite beautiful up here. It reminds me of San Francisco. I really miss home.

Soyeong It must be so nice for you to go back. **Are you all ready to go?**

Alex Yes. I packed my suitcases this morning and I'm ready to go! **I wish you could be there with me.**

Soyeong Me, too. But it's only for two weeks.

Alex Still, I feel sorry that you can't make it with me this time.

Soyeong **Don't worry.** There will be other times. **Say hello to your mother for me.**

Key Patterns

1. I feel sorry that _____.
   I feel sorry that you can't make it with me this time.

2. That used to be _____.
   That used to be the tallest building in Korea.

3. Where is _____?
   Where is the famous 63 building?

1

I feel sorry that _____. _____ 해서 유감입니다.
I feel sorry that you can't make it with me this time.

동감, 즉 상대편에 대해서 자신의 감정을 표현할 때 I feel sorry를 사용했습니다. 상대편이 가엾거나 안타깝게 느껴질 때 감정을 나타내는 표현이지요. 가장 먼저 I feel sorry for _____ 그리고 I feel sorry that _____ 표현부터 익혀봅시다.

I feel sorry for her husband. 그녀의 남편이 참 안됐어요.
I feel sorry that she was left behind. 남겨진 그녀가 참 안됐어요.

이번에는 sorry 대신 다른 형용사를 넣어서 배운 내용을 활용해봅시다. I feel + 형용사 표현입니다.

I feel dizzy. I feel terrible. 어지러워요. 좀 기분이 안 좋은데요.
I'm feeling better. 훨씬 좋아졌어요.
She feels responsible for her kid's behavior.
그녀는 자식의 행동에 책임감을 느꼈어요.

160

2

That used to be _____.　과거에 _____ 였습니다.

That used to be the tallest building in Korea.

That/it used to + 동사는 예전에 그랬다는 표현으로 사용합니다. Used to는 과거의 사실이나 상태, 혹은 규칙적인 습관을 나타낼 때 사용하죠.

There used to be only four subway lines in Seoul.

예전에 서울에는 지하철 노선이 4개밖에 없었어요.

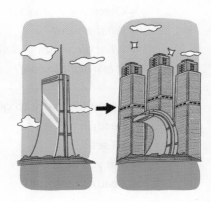

물론 사람이 주어로 올 수 있습니다.

She used to be a ballerina.　그녀는 발레리나였어요.
They used to date.　그들은 과거에 데이트를 했던 사이다.

3

Where is _____?

_____ 는 어디에 있나요?

Where is the famous 63 Building?

"Where 동사 + 주어?"는 모르는 장소를 찾을 때 유용하게 사용할 수 있습니다. 특히 해외여행 영어에서 필수라고 할 수 있겠습니다.

Where are you?　너 지금 어디 있니?
Where is SangAm World Cup Stadium?

상암 월드컵 경기장은 어디에 있습니까?

Alternative Expressions

1 Look at that view!
= *Check out that view!*
= *What a view!*
= *What an amazing view!*
= *It is a sight to see!*

2 Are you all ready to go?
= *Ready?*
= *All set?*
= *Are you all set?*
= *Ready to take off?*

3 I wish you could be there with me.
Too bad you can't make it.
I'm sorry that you can't make it.
Sorry you have to miss the event/the trip.

4 Don't worry.
For reassurance:
It's okay.
No worries.
It'll be fine.
For problems to solve:
No sweat.
No problem.

5 Say hello to your mother for me.

= *Give my regards to your mother.*

= *Say hello to your mother for me.*

= *Give her a hug for me.*

= *Kiss the babies for me.*

= *Tell her I said hello.*

= *If you see her, say hello.*

Focus on Pronunciation

복합어 강세 – 강세에 따른 의미 변화

형용사 + 명사 = 복합어인 경우 형용사에 강세를 두며,
형용사 + 명사 = 명사구인 경우 명사에 강세를 두어 발음합니다.

English teacher 영어 선생님
English teacher 영국인 선생님
the White House 백악관
white house 하얀 집

1. 만나 뵙게 되어서 좋았습니다. It was really good meeting you.

헤어지면서 사용할 수 있는 표현들 중 가장 많이 사용하는 말이죠. "Goodbye"라는 간단한 인사만 하기보다는 상대방에게 좀 더 호감을 주고 대화를 마무리할 수 있는 좋은 표현입니다. 만나서 좋았다는 건 현재가 아닌 과거를 표현하는 말로 과거시제를 사용하여 is의 과거형인 was를 썼다는 점 유의하세요.

> A: It's time for me to go. It was really good meeting you.
> B: Yes, we must do this again soon. Bye.

2. 가끔 네 생각이 날 거야. I'm really going to/gonna miss you.

헤어질 때 사용하는 아주 다정한 표현입니다. Going to는 줄여서 구어체에서는 gonna 라고 짧게 사용할 수 있습니다. 발음하기도 훨씬 수월하답니다. 이 표현은 '나중에 당신이 그리워질 거예요' 라는 뜻이니까, 첫 번째 표현과 마찬가지로 그냥 See you! Bye! 대신에 꼭 한번 사용해보세요. 상대방의 반응이 정말 다르다는 것을 실감하실 수 있을 겁니다.

> A: Everything is all packed and I'm ready to go on my trip.
> B: OK, take care. I'm really going to miss you!

3. 모든 일이 순조롭기를 바랍니다. I hope you do well.

대개 행운을 빈다, 혹은 파이팅을 좀 더 정중하게 말하고자 할 때 쓰는 표현입니다. 우리도 누군가에게 위로나 힘이 되고플 때, 장기간 떨어져 있을 때 이렇게 말하죠. 이 표현은 '다 잘될거야'의 의미로도 사용할 수 있습니다. 기본적으로 I hope~으로 문장을 시작하면 '~을 기원하다, ~바라다'라는 뜻을 나타내기 때문에 격식을 갖춘 표현이 됩니다. 여러분께 제가 하고픈 말이기도 하네요. 여러분 모두 Real & Live를 통해 유용하고 재밌는 표현 많이 배우셨기를 바라며 하시는 모든 일이 잘 되길 바랍니다.

A: I just wanted to say goodbye.
   I'm leaving next week to try out for the Olympics at the international qualifying competition.
B: That's wonderful. I hope you do well.

Exercises

1. (   ) Matthew is not a heavy drinker.

2. (   ) Everyone brings food to a potluck dinner.

3. (   ) Michael is a theater director from Canada.

4. (   ) Alex can talk directly to Liz over the phone.

5. (   ) Soyeong works in the financial industry in Seoul.

6. (   ) Alex and Soyeong do not have anything in common.

7. (   ) Michael's new play impressed both Soyeong and Alex.

8. (   ) Ben confused the pronunciation of "snacks" with "snakes".

9. (   ) Alex and Soyeong are not able to attend Michael's birthday party.

10. (   ) Soyeong feels sorry that she cannot visit San Francisco with Alex.

11. (   ) Michael cannot make a reservation at the first hotel over the phone.

12. (   ) Stella says the best way to improve English ability is to use language in real life.

The Northeast: The wealthiest region, in the United States, this area includes historic states such as New York, New Jersey and Massachusetts. The Northeast played a dominant role in the founding of America. Some of the states are referred to as the "New England" region, indicating the British origin of the country's earliest settlers.

The Northwest
The Midwest
The Northeast
The South
The Southwest

The American South, or "The South":
Given the history of the Civil War (1861~1865) in which the South was opposed to the North, the South has developed its own rich and distinctive customs, literature, music and food. Historically, the South was an area that produced huge plantations of cotton, tobacco and rice. African Americans have a long and important history in the South, including the tragic legacy of slavery in America.

Midwestern United States or "The Midwest": This broad expanse of area includes such states as Michigan, Illinois, Nebraska and Kansas. The city of Chicago and the famous Mississippi River were important for trading and the transportation of crops. Flat, prairie land covers most of the states west of the Mississippi River and thus, many of the states are part of what is called the "Great Plains." Since this area is in the central part of the country, it is also called the "heartland" of America.

Southwestern United States or "The Southwest": This dry, desert region consists of states like Arizona, New Mexico, Texas, Southern California, and Nevada. There is a strong presence of Spanish – speaking peoples and a strong Mexican heritage. The area is known for its hot and dry climate. The world – famous Grand Canyon, a tremendous gorge carved out by the Colorado River, is located in the state of Arizona.

The Northwest or "Pacific Northwest": This area usually refers to states along the northern part of the West Coast such as Washington, Oregon and the area of northern California. Since it is along the Pacific Ocean, these states are part of the "Pacific Northwest." Cities like Seattle are famous for the amount of rain; the region is known for being damp and wet. The term "Northwest" can also refer to Idaho, Montana, and Wyoming.

● **What is the oldest and wealthiest region of America called?**

● **Which region has a strong presence of Spanish - speaking peoples?**

Exercise Answer Key

• **Lesson 1   Select the Appropriate Word**

1. a (like)   2. b (quite)   3. b (to meet)

4. a (do)   5. a (at)   6. b (Let's)   7. a (for)

• **Lesson 2   Match Up Words and Meaning**

1. E   2. C   3. A   4. J   5. F

6. D   7. B   8. I   9. H   10. G

• **Lesson 3   Choosing the Word**

1. come here   2. used to   3. tell me   4. playing   5. love

6. favorite   7. fun   8. coincidence   9. would you like   10. sounds

---

• **Lesson 4   Crossword Puzzle**

Down

1. impressed
2. backstage
4. lovely
5. scene
7. autograph

Across

3. famous
6. favorite
8. excellent
9. director
10. especially

• **Lesson 5   Error Correction**

1. What's Seoul like?
2. I was impressed.

3. Thanks for coming.

4. I'm so happy for you.

5. You're such a good girl.

6. May I take a message?

7. What do you think about movies?

8. Let's all get together lunch.

9. Why don't we go backstage and say hello to Michael?

10. I would like to tell touch base about her visit in Seoul.

• Lesson 6   Select the Appropriate Word

1. a (autograph)   2. b (called)   3. b (gorgeous)   4. b (going to a movie)
5. a (delicate, sweet)   6. b (calling)   7. a (exciting)

• Lesson 7   Collocation Match Up

1. look so cute
2. thanks for ~ing
3. sound like fun
4. take a message
5. make sure

6. put through
7. look forward to ~ing
8. hold my liquor
9. stick with
10. cut down on

• Lesson 8   Grammar Practice

1. a. through   b. in   c. like   d. from   e. for   f. to
2. a. crowded   b. confusing   c. looking   d. coming   e. eating   f. said

• Lesson 9   Find the errors and make corrections

1. What are you eating?

2. I think, I am confused.

3. How much are these?

4. It's a great place to shop (for shopping).

5. Why do you look so sick?

6. If you don't use it, you will lose it.

7. That's a great way to study English.

8. Matthew and I went bar hopping last night.

9. I have been watching English class on OUN – TV.

10. I either have to cut down on my drinking or not drink at all.

• Lesson 10 Match Up Words and Meaning

1. F   2. I   3. E   4. D   5. B

6. C   7. G   8. J   9. A   10. H

• Lesson 11 Crossword Puzzle

Down

1. present
2. hope
4. celebrate
8. drink

Across

3. bring
5. scare
6. surprise
7. birthday
9. comfortable
10. travel

• Lesson 12 Choosing the Word

1. free time
2. something to eat
3. Let's see
4. would
5. go for anything

6. feel like
7. would be fine
8. prefer
9. how to use
10. also

• Lesson 13 Grammar practice

1. a. for   b. on   c. with   d. in   e. for   f. on
2. a. going   b. knew   c. planning   d. seen   e. thinking   f. using

• Lesson 14 Reorder Sentences

⑦ — ⑤ — ③ — ① — ④ — ⑥ — ⑧ — ②

• Lesson 15 True or False

1. F   7. T
2. T   8. T
3. T   9. F
4. F   10. F
5. F   11. T
6. F   12. T

Korean Translation

• Lesson 1

[지하철역 입구]

소영: 제니퍼! 여기서 뭐하고 있어요?

제니퍼: 오, 소영씨, 제 친구 만나려고 하고 있어요. 여기 제 친구를 소개할게요. 마이크! 이
쪽은 전에 제 한국어 선생님이었던 친구예요.

소영: 안녕하세요, 저는 소영이라고 합니다. 만나서 반갑습니다.

마이클: 제 이름은 마이클입니다. 소영씨, 만나서 반갑습니다. 여기 서울에서 뭐하세요?

소영: 저는 한국방송통신대학교 학생이에요.

마이클: 영어를 참 잘하시네요. 미국이나 캐나다에서 사신 적이 있으세요?

소영: 애리조나에서 3년 정도 공부했어요.

마이클: 애리조나라구요! 흥미롭네요. 애리조나는 어떻습니까?

소영: 더워요! 하지만 그곳은 정말 좋았어요.

제니퍼: 우리 다시 만나서, 얘기를 나누면 좋겠어요. 우리 언제 함께 커피 마셔요.

마이클: 좋은 생각이에요! 여기, 제 명함이에요.

소영: 감사합니다.

• Lesson 2

제니퍼: 다들 잘 지냈죠? 늦어서 미안해요.

소영: 괜찮아요. 어디서 오는 길이에요?

제니퍼: 이태원에서 제 남자친구 만나서 점심을 먹었거든요. 이렇게 교통이 복잡할 것이라
고 생각 못했어요.

마이클: 만나고 있는 사람이 있는지 몰랐어요. 남자친구 사진 있어요?

제니퍼: 그럼요, 휴대전화에 있어요.

소영: 아, 남자친구하고 잘 어울려요. 부러워요.

마이클: 당신은요? 만나는 사람 없어요?

소영: 아니요. 전 아직 혼자예요. 저도 남자친구가 있었으면 좋겠어요.

제니퍼: 당신은 꼭 좋은 사람 만날 거예요. 당신이 얼마나 매력적인데요. 관심 가는 사람은 없어요?

소영: 음... 찾고 있기는 한데 특별히 관심 있는 사람은 없어요.

마이클: 만약 당신이 사람 만나는 것에 관심이 있으시다면, 제가 소개팅을 주선해보죠. 어떤 남자를 좋아하세요?

• Lesson 3

소영: 굉장히 좋은 식당이네요!

알렉스: 네, 제가 좋아하는 곳입니다. 나와주셔서 감사합니다. 이렇게 만나 뵙는군요. 마이클에게서 소영씨에 대해서는 많은 이야기를 들었습니다.

소영: 그러세요? 저는 당신에 대해 별로 아는 것이 없는데... 혹시, 실례가 안 된다면, 무슨 일을 하시는지 여쭤봐도 될까요?

알렉스: 아, 네, 저는 금융쪽 일을 하고 있어요.

소영: 아, 재미있으시겠어요.

알렉스: 글쎄요. 금융과 관련된 일을 하고 있지만, 제가 정말 좋아하는 분야는 연극이에요. 소영씨는 주로 시간 있을 때는 뭐하세요?

소영: 아, 저도 연극 좋아해요. 사실 저는 저희 대학 연극반에서 활동하고 있어요.

알렉스: 우연의 일치군요! 저도 대학 다닐 때 연극을 좀 한 적이 있어요. 뮤지컬은 좋아하세요?

소영: 뮤지컬은 정말 멋지죠! 마이클이 소개해줬는데, 정말 좋았어요. 뮤지컬을 좀 더 자주 볼 수 있으면 좋겠어요.

알렉스: 마이클이 연출하는 새 뮤지컬 표 두 장을 줬어요. 대학로인데요. 이번 주말에 같이 보러 가지 않을래요?

소영: 좋아요! 제 일정 좀 확인해보고요, 마침 이번주에 시간이 되는데요, 언제쯤 만날까요?

[공연 후]

알렉스: 음...공연 어땠어요?

소영: 정말 좋았어요. 당신은 어땠어요?

알렉스: 아, 저도 감동받았습니다. 마지막 장면이 제일 인상적이었습니다.

소영: 그래요. 연기도 노래도 정말 좋았어요.

알렉스: 특히 노래가요. 그 여배우는 정말 환상적이었어요.

소영: 그렇죠. 그녀의 목소리는 정말 사랑스러워요. 마이클이 자부할 만해요. 연출력이 정
말 놀라웠어요.

알렉스: 우리 무대 뒤로 가서 마이클한테 인사할까요?

소영: 물론이죠. 재미있겠는걸요.

[무대 뒤]

마이클: 아, 소영씨, 알렉스!! 와주었군요, 감사합니다. 어땠어요?

소영: 와우! 우리 둘 다 너무 감동받았습니다. 마이클씨는 이제 유명한 연출가시네요!

알렉스: 그러게요, 여기 사인 좀 해주실 수 있겠습니까?

마이클: 물론, 기쁜 마음으로 해드리지요!

메리: 좋은 아침입니다. 스미스필드 회사입니다. 무엇을 도와드릴까요?

알렉스: 안녕하세요, 저는 한국의 알렉스 최인데, 리즈 채프먼과 통화하고 싶습니다.

메리: 죄송합니다. 채프먼씨는 지금 사무실에 계시지 않습니다. 메모를 남겨드릴까요?

알렉스: 네, 그럼, 다음주 채프먼씨의 서울 방문과 관련해서 전화를 드렸다고 전해주세요.
채프먼씨가 언제쯤 사무실에 돌아오실 것 같은가요?

메리: 아마 한 시간 이내에는 들어오실 것 같습니다.

알렉스: 알겠습니다. 그러면 그녀가 돌아오면 전화 좀 부탁 드려주세요.

메리: 잘 알겠습니다. 혹시 성을 다시 말씀해주시겠습니까?

알렉스: 네, 최입니다. C-H-O-I 입니다.

메리: 감사합니다. 채프먼씨가 확실히 전달받을 수 있도록 하겠습니다.

알렉스의 비서: 한국 금융증권입니다. 무엇을 도와드릴까요?

리즈: 안녕하세요, 저 리즈 채프먼입니다. 알렉스 최와 통화하고 싶습니다.

알렉스의 비서: 잠깐만 기다려주십시오. 연결해드리겠습니다.

알렉스: 리즈, 잘 지내셨어요? 제 연락 받으셨죠?

리즈: 안녕하세요! 알렉스! 서울에서 다음주에 만나 뵙는 것을 기대하고 있습니다. 우리는
     상의해야 할 흥미로운 일들이 많잖아요.

Lesson 6

리즈: 멋져요! 이곳은 뭐라고 부르죠?

알렉스: 여기는 인사동이에요. 한국의 전통 시장이죠. 여기서 당신의 아이들을 위한 선물을
     살 수 있을 거예요. 이곳은 매우 붐비기는 하지만, 기념품을 사기에 좋은 장소거든요.

리즈: 네. 여긴 정말 사람이 많네요. 어머, 너무 아름다워요! 이것들은 무엇이죠?

알렉스: 그것들은 한국 전통 인형이에요.

리즈: 사랑스러워요. 정말 사랑스러워요. 인형들이 우아하고 화려하군요.

가게 주인: 무엇을 도와드릴까요?

알렉스: 그냥 구경하는 거예요. 감사합니다.

가게 주인: 만약 필요한 것이 있으면 말씀하세요.

리즈: 저것들은 무엇이죠?

알렉스: 그것들은 한국 전통 과자와 사탕이에요. 저것들은 얼마인가요?

가게 주인: 3천 원입니다.

리즈: 좋네요! 각각 한 개씩 주세요.

소영: 왜 그렇게 아파 보여요?

알렉스: 티 많이 나요? 지난밤에 일 끝나고 술을 너무 많이 마셨나봐요.

마이클: 당신도요? 저는 어제 매튜와 술집을 돌아다녔어요. 전 폭탄주를 너무 많이 마셨는
지 숙취가 있네요.

매튜: 네. 술고래처럼 마셨죠. 아, 너무 큰 실수예요. 술 좋아해요?

소영: 저요? 아니요. 저는 술을 잘 못해요.

알렉스: 전 폭탄주는 못 마시겠어요. 그건 저한텐 너무 독해요. 전 보통 맥주를 마셔요.

마이클: 네, 과음하면 다음날 아침에 일어났을 때 너무 고통스러워요. 알렉스는 지난밤에
많이 취했어요?

알렉스: 아니요. 다행히도 오늘 아침 스프를 마실 수 있었어요. 그것은 내 속을 안정시키는
데 도움이 되거든요.

소영: 만약 속이 괜찮다면, 액체를 많이 마시는 것 역시 도움이 될 거예요.

매튜: 그렇죠. 그런 이야기를 들은 적 있어요. 전 술을 줄이거나 술을 끊어야 할 것 같아요.
술이 항상 제 속을 아프게 하거든요.

소영: 그거 정말 좋은 생각인걸요!

벤: 소영씨, 안녕! 뭘 먹고 있어요?

소영: 스텔라 선생님께서 먹을 것을 좀 가져오셨어요.

벤: 뭐라구요? 다시 말씀해줄래요?

소영: 간식거리(snacks)요. 왜 그러시는데요?

벤: 어, 잠깐만요. 저 좀 헷갈려서, "뱀(snacks)"을 말씀하시는 거예요?

소영: 간식거리(snacks)요, 식사와 식사 사이에 먹는 음식이요. 예를 들면, 크래커나 칩, 쿠
키, 뭐 그런 종류들 있잖아요.

벤: 아, 간식거리요~ 저는 소영씨가 "뱀"이라고 말하는 줄 알았어요. 그 발음이 가끔 혼란
스러워요. 발음의 차이를 구분하는 것이 사실 좀 어려워요.

스텔라: 두 사람은 무슨 얘기를 하면서 그렇게 웃고 있어요?

소영: 벤이 제가 "스낵(간식거리)" 대신 "뱀(snacks)"이라고 말한 줄 알았대요.

스텔라: 그렇죠, 발음은 정말 혼란스러울 수 있어요.

벤: 가끔, 단어의 발음과 뜻의 차이를 구분하는 것은 정말 어려워요.

스텔라: 그럼, 오늘 우리 수업시간에, 발음을 향상시키는 방법에 대해서 이야기해보지요.

• Lesson 9

스텔라: 자, 말해봅시다. 여러분은 영어 발음을 어떻게 연습하고 있어요?

소영: OUN-TV 영어강좌하고, 영어 자막이 있는 미국 TV 쇼를 보고 있어요.

스텔라: 좋은 생각이에요. 미국 TV 쇼를 본 적 있나요? 그것은 영어 공부를 하는 데 매우 좋은 방법이에요.

메간: 저는 일 때문에 TV 볼 시간이 없어요. 대신 영어 대화를 MP3로 다운받아서, 버스나 지하철 타고 다닐 때 들어요.

스텔라: 그래요? 통근 시간을 제대로 활용하고 있군요. 또 어떤 방법이 있을까요? 영어를 향상시킬 수 있는 다른 방법을 알려주세요.

에릭: 저는 영어로 된 신문과 잡지를 읽는 방법을 통해 배울 수 있도록 노력하고 있어요.

스텔라: 역시 좋은 학습 방법들입니다. 새로운 단어를 발견하면 꼭 기억하도록 하세요.

벤: 영어를 사용하는 친구를 사귀는 것도 도움이 돼요.

스텔라: 맞아요. 실제 생활에서 영어를 사용하는 것이 영어를 향상시키는 데 제일 좋은 방법이에요. 기억하세요. 사용하지 않으면, 잊어버립니다!

• Lesson 10

마이클: 잘 지내죠? 혹시 둘 다 이번 주말에 시간 있어요? 우리 집에서 몇몇 친구들과 저녁을 먹을까 생각 중이에요.

알렉스: 미안합니다. 참석할 수 없을 것 같아요. 저는 이번 주말에 선약이 있습니다.

소영: 참석하고 싶지만, 저도 갈 수가 없네요. 전 다음주에 기말시험이 있어서 주말 내내

벼락공부를 해야 해요. 미안해요.

마이클: 괜찮아요. 이해해요. 그럼 다음에 하죠.

알렉스: 그럼요, 물론이죠! 음, 소영과 저는 친구 선물을 사러 가야겠습니다.

마이클: 그래요. 다음에 봐요.

제니퍼: 마이클! 잘 지내죠? 무슨 일이에요?

마이클: 제니퍼, 들어봐요. 혹시 당신과 매튜가 이번 주말에 저녁 먹으러 우리 집에 올 수 있을까요?

제니퍼: 물론이죠. 우리는 당연히 돼요. 그런데 무슨 일 있어요? 목소리가 조금 우울하게 들리는데요.

마이클: 예, 지금 좀 기분이 안 좋아요. 솔직히 말해, 내 생일이라 소영과 알렉스에게 축하를 받고 싶었는데, 그들이 올 수 없대요. 아무도 참석하지 않을 것 같아요. 당신은 확실히 올 수 있는 거죠?

제니퍼: 저는 갈 수 있어요. 절대 잊지 않을게요! 저를 초대해줘서 고마워요. 혹시 제가 가져갈 것이 있나요?

마이클: 당신만 오면 돼요. 아무것도 가지고 올 필요 없어요!

• Lesson 11

제니퍼와 매튜: 어이! 생일 축하해요!

마이클: 안녕, 친구들! 어서 들어와요. 와줘서 고마워요.

제니퍼: 여기, 우리가 당신을 위해 준비했어요. 작은 건데 당신 마음에 들었으면 좋겠네요.

마이클: 와우. 이런 것은 가져오지 않아도 되는데. 와, 여행 책자네요! 이건 내가 찾던 거예요! 고마워요.

[현관벨이 울리면서 마이클이 소영과 알렉스를 맞이한다]

마이클: 소영? 알렉스? 여기는 어쩐 일이에요?

소영과 알렉스: 깜짝 놀랐지!

마이클: 무슨 일이에요?

소영: 우린 당신 생일인 것 알고 있었어요. 우린 단지 당신을 깜짝 놀라게 해주고 싶었어

요! 여기 선물이에요.

알렉스: 여기도 있습니다. 이것도 당신 선물이예요.

마이클: 정말 믿을 수가 없군요! 고마워요! 어서 들어와요! 편히 앉아서 마음껏 즐겨요!

소영: 우리가 당신을 놀라게 한 건 아닌가 모르겠네요. 어서 축하하자구요!

마이클: 와줘서 너무 고마워요, 정말. 자 다들 마시죠!

• Lesson 12

제니퍼: 마이클! 이거 어디에 놓을까요? 저는 와인과 치즈를 가지고 왔어요.

마이클: 멋져요! 식당에 테이블이 있어요. 거기에 올려놓으면 돼요.

알렉스: 너무 배가 고픈데요! 전 뭔가 저를 채워줄 것이 필요해요.

소영: 당신은 이것들을 좀 먹는 게 좋겠군요. 보세요. 제가 김밥을 가지고 왔어요.

마이클: 자! 모두들. 주방에 약간의 샐러드와 파스타를 준비했어요. 마음껏 드세요.

제니퍼: 파스타요? 맛있겠는데요!

[모든 사람들이 부엌으로 이동한다]

소영: 이 파스타 냄새가 매우 좋은데요. 그리고 이 토마토들은 매우 신선하네요!

제니퍼: 음, 이 파스타는 제가 먹어본 중에 제일 맛있어요. 마이클, 당신은 멋진 요리사군요!

알렉스: 자! 와인을 따자구요! 그리고 누가 저에게 스파게티 접시 좀 주시겠어요?

마이클: 지난주에 숙취 때문에 고생한 지 얼마 되지 않았는데 정말 술을 마실 수 있겠어요?

알렉스: 이건 파티잖아요! 그리고 어쨌든, 하루 한 잔의 와인은 건강에 좋다구요.

• Lesson 13

마이클: 알렉스, 혹시 휴가 계획은?

알렉스: 저는 몇 주 동안 샌프란시스코에 가려고요. 저랑 함께 가실 분 있으신가요?

마이클: 저는 휴가 기간에 한국에 있을 계획이에요. 그런데 어디로 갈지를 아직 못 정했어요. 추천할 만한 곳이 있나요?

소영: 음... 부산에 가본 적이 있어요?

마이클: 아니요. 그곳에 가면 무엇을 볼 수 있죠?

알렉스: 제 생각에, 당신은 해운대 해변을 꼭 다녀와야 해요.

소영: 맞아요. 그곳에 가지 않고는 부산 여행을 했다고 할 수 없죠. 그곳의 해산물은 매우 신선하고 맛있어요. 언제 갈 예정이에요?

마이클: 이번 달 안에 갈 생각이에요.

알렉스: 휴가는 몇 일이나 있을 예정이에요?

마이클: 일주일 정도요.

알렉스: 그러면 편의를 위해 예약을 하는 게 좋겠어요. 휴가 기간엔 사람이 매우 많거든요.

소영: 네, 거기서 호텔을 예약하려고 하는 것보다 지금 예약하는 게 좋겠어요. 제가 도와드 릴게요.

- **Lesson 14**

호텔 직원 A: 안녕하세요. 해운대 호텔 예약부 비키입니다. 무엇을 도와드릴까요?

마이클: 네, 17일에 예약을 할 수 있을까요?

호텔 직원 A: 네, 가능합니다. 총 몇 분이신가요? 저희는 싱글룸, 더블룸, 스위트룸이 있습 니다.

마이클: 저 혼자입니다.

호텔 직원 A: 그러면 몇 일간 머무르실 예정인가요?

마이클: 21일까지 묵고 싶습니다.

호텔 직원 A: 죄송합니다. 손님. 20일 이후로는 모두 예약이 완료되었습니다. 제가 다른 호텔을 소개시켜드려도 괜찮을까요?

호텔 직원 B: 부산호텔입니다. 무엇을 도와드릴까요?

마이클: 안녕하세요. 17일부터 21일까지 싱글룸 있습니까? 그리고 저는 바다가 보이는 방 에 묵고 싶습니다.

호텔 직원 B: 잠시만 기다려주세요. 손님. 제가 확인해보겠습니다. 네, 말씀하신 날짜에 숙 박하실 수 있습니다. 예약해드릴까요 손님?

마이클: 네, 부탁합니다.

호텔 직원 B: 이번 달 17일에서 21일까지 총 4박 하시고, 바다 전망의 싱글룸입니다. 그리고 17일 몇 시경에 체크인할 예정이신가요? 오전, 오후, 저녁 중 언제인가요?

마이클: 저는 오후 중에 체크인할 예정입니다.

• Lesson 15

알렉스: 저기 봐요!

소영: 멋지지 않아요? 저기가 명동이에요!

알렉스: 오, 맞아요. 저기네요. 그 유명한 63빌딩은 어디죠?

소영: 그건 저기예요. 예전에 한국에서 제일 높은 빌딩이었어요.

알렉스: 여기는 매우 아름답네요. 이곳은 샌프란시스코를 생각나게 해요. 고향집이 매우 그립네요.

소영: 돌아가면 매우 좋을 거예요. 당신 돌아갈 준비는 다 된 거예요?

알렉스: 네. 오늘 아침 가방을 모두 챙겼어요. 갈 준비는 끝났어요! 당신이 나와 함께 가주면 좋을 텐데요.

소영: 저도 그래요. 하지만 겨우 2주간이잖아요.

알렉스: 이번에 당신과 함께 가지 못해 아쉬워요.

소영: 걱정말아요. 다음에 기회가 있을 거예요. 당신 어머니께 안부 전해주세요.

집 | 필 | 자

박 윤 주

이화여자대학교 사범대학 영어교육과 학사
미국 The Ohio State University 영어교육학 석사
미국 Indiana University 영어교육학 박사

● 현재 : 한국방송통신대학교 영어영문학과 조교수
　　　　OUN-TV(방송대학 TV)「영어회화 1, 2」,「박윤주의 영어회화」 진행
　　　　EBS e-TV(교육방송)「박윤주의 Classroom English」 진행

찰 스 윤

미국 University of Wisconsin, Madison 영어영문학 학사
미국 University of Illinois, Urbana-Champaign 동아시아학 석사

● 현재 : 한국방송통신대학교 영어영문학과 객원교수

◆ 한국방송통신대학교 영어영문학과
　http://eng.knou.ac.kr (02)3668-4560